Book Tveir - The Prophecy Unravels
Anna Pattison

Copyright © 2025 by Anna Pattison

All rights reserved.

No part of this publication may be reproduced, distributed, or transmitted in any form or by any means, including photocopying, recording, or other electronic or mechanical methods, without the prior written permission of the publisher, except as permitted by U.S. copyright law. For permission requests, contact Anna Pattison

The story, all names, characters, and incidents portrayed in this production are fictitious. No identification with actual persons (living or deceased), places, buildings, and products is intended or should be inferred.

Book Cover by TabGraphix

Dedicated

to The Lady, *Vanadis*

Contents

Books In The Norse Prophecy Series — VI
Prologue — 1
Epigraph — 3
1. Chapter One — 5
2. Chapter Two — 11
3. Chapter Three — 15
4. Chapter Four — 23
5. Chapter Five — 31
6. Chapter Six — 35
7. Chapter Seven — 39
8. Chapter Eight — 43
9. Chapter Nine — 49
10. Chapter Ten — 53
11. Chapter Eleven — 59
12. Chapter Twelve — 63
13. Chapter Thirteen — 69

14.	Chapter Fourteen	79
15.	Chapter Fifteen	85
16.	Chapter Sixteen	89
17.	Chapter Seventeen	97
18.	Chapter Eighteen	101
19.	Chapter Nineteen	107
20.	Chapter Twenty	113
21.	Chapter Twenty-One	123
22.	Chapter Twenty-Two	127
23.	Chapter Twenty-Three	135
24.	Chapter Twenty-Four	143
25.	Chapter Twenty-Five	151
26.	Chapter Twenty-Six	157
27.	Chapter Twenty-Seven	163
28.	Chapter Twenty-Eight	177
29.	Chapter Twent-Nine	181
Afterword		187
Acknowledgements		188

BOOKS IN THE NORSE PROPHECY SERIES

Book Ein – Prophecy of Love

Book Tveir – The Prophecy Unravels

Book Prir – Prophecy Transformed

As the ship sighted their shores Sven swiftly let out a breath of relief. He had successfully experienced his first viking. He and many of the village men had voyaged to explore beyond their shores. He had fought, raided, hunted, and returned safely. Now all he wanted was the quiet farming life until spring planting was done and he could join another viking. He glimpsed Freyja riding along the beach and readied himself nervously. He knew he had a duty to be with her, but the fire that she had kindled within his belly had been slowly dying over these months at sea and exploring. Still, he could not help feeling excited watching her body move, her well-muscled thighs griping her horse tightly as she rode. For a moment he mused about "the mighty passion" or *"inn matki munr"*, but the captain approached shaking him free from his thoughts.

"You now have a new responsibility to the village," the captain shouted above the raucous breaking waves. "You will guard our captive, the Far Isle chief's daughter. No harm will befall her, no man will lay hands upon her. *You would not want to touch things you should not touch.*" The captain directed a stern look at Sven. "You will swear to this?"

Sven sighed deeply, wanting only his farm. "Yes, Gunnar, I hear you."

"The village prosperity depends upon you. The prophecy says, 'When Freyja and Sven couple and children are born then we will trade with many and our village will prosper.' Who is to say that ransom is not also trade?" chuckled the captain with a shrug as he walked away.

When Freyja greeted Sven on the beach, he accepted her volcanic passion as had been his habit all throughout their relationship. In one swift impetuous movement Freyja pulled Sven behind a driftwood log barely offering cover. She was like a Valkyrie and he a fallen warrior who stepped off his boat to be taken. He was a willing victim to her aggressions as she yearned to resume their love making. She had let her passion escape and gave herself wholeheartedly, as she took his desire. Her breath quickened at his touch and she thrilled as they met in hurried ecstasy. He was caught up in sensations, abandoning himself to the dance of their bodies.

In the afterglow they had walked together, ankle deep into the frothy waves, to wash off. Sven did not know what to say and Freyja did not ask for words.

"When Freyja and Sven couple
and children are born
then we will trade with many
and our village will prosper."

Chapter One

They walked alongside her horse laden with the spoils of the safely returned voyager, Sven. Freyja gripped tightly to her warrior's arm feeling warmed by his body and the passion shared on the beach. She smiled up at him proudly. Sven was now indeed a warrior as he had returned from his first viking. The explorations and raids had gone well. The men had returned with many skins and treasures. Freyja and Sven could now look forward to spending winter together. To fill the long cold nights with their love making and bring their prophecy into reality.

Freyja thought back on the past spring when she had taken Sven and he had responded in kind. She had realized that if she was for Sven, the reciprocal might also be true, Sven was for her. This idea had thrilled her with a new sense of purpose and power. She could be the huntress and no longer had to wait for Sven to come to her. They had certainly discovered the release of their passion with each other and Freyja longed to learn more of their bodies' potential together. She desperately hoped that Sven would soon be ready to live under the same roof and begin their family.

As they walked the sandy path to the village, they each looked forward to the celebration ahead. Freyja was eager for all to witness the reality of the two of them together; the couple to fulfill the prophecy. Sven simply hoped to see his parents and share tales of the expedition. As he thought about this the captain walked back to remind Sven again of his new responsibilities, "Do not forget that you have more important things to do than farming, right now." Freyja smiled up at Sven proudly. He was now indeed more than a farmer.

When Freyja and Sven reached the village, the celebration had already begun. The triumphant voyagers were being greeted by their women and children. Discoveries and spoils were being divided and Sven unloaded the horse to do the same. His parents arrived and were awarded with the things he had brought back. Freyja waited with an eager smile of anticipation on her face, her hands outstretched, for a token.

Sven's parents greeted Freyja, with reserved nods as always, then put their arms around Sven and steered him into the Mead House. They held on to him and patted his back, all the time laughing and speaking happily about his return and their rich gifts. Freyja scowled with the idea that they had not included her, but said nothing. She waited outside for her mother.

Soon the figures in dark cloaks were escorted into the Mead House by two men. While racing to greet Sven she had seen them leave the ship. From the corner of her eye, she had barely glimpsed them as she wrapped her arms and legs about him in passionate welcome.

From inside the Mead House, Freyja heard the captain yell to Sven unceremoniously, "Greet your parents and then you will sit near the black-haired daughter, to guard her." Freyja turned to look through the open door but could make out nothing in the darkness.

"My daughter," Freyja heard Arndis call out. "Where is Sven?"

"He is inside with his parents telling stories, but I wanted to wait for you," Freyja lied.

"Well, let us join them. We are all family now," her mother said in a happy tone. "I have brought you your pretty new shawl for the chilly walk home, though I know you will be warm in Sven's arms." She pressed the prized possession into Freyja's arms with an almost girlish giggle.

The women entered the Mead House, warmed from many bodies and the fire. They joined Sven and the others for free-flowing mead and stories. There was acting out of their many adventures and much laughter. Soon all were in wonderful moods. After a time, the men who had families, started to leave with their women and children. Arndis said her good nights with a wink to Freyja and Sven. Freyja walked to the door with her while Arndis whispered promises that she would not disturb them in the night or the morning, smiling very cheerfully. The older villagers soon drifted off and only the young people were left.

Freyja turned back from the doorway to find Sven sitting alone near the fire watching the two strangers. The two had taken off their hoods to reveal they were women with shockingly dark hair. One appeared younger than Sven and was very beautiful. She had an ivory complexion and rose-colored lips. The other was matronly and seemed intent on caring for the younger. They had eaten well and seemed to be almost asleep at the table.

"Come with me, now," Freyja pulled Sven by the arm with a smile. "It is time we were asleep as well. My bed is warm with many skins and waits for us." She placed Sven's cool hand upon her warm breast. Her eyes twinkled with the promise.

Sven pulled his arm away saying, "No, I will stay here. The captain said I must watch the captives."

"But, Sven, the others can watch them. We can be together now," Freyja smiled seductively.

"No, I will stay," Sven replied his gaze fixed on the younger woman.

An unfamiliar feeling rose inside of Freyja. She was hurt, she was angry, she was... jealous. For no logical reason, she was being refused by Sven. It did not make sense and she did not know what to do. She stood in front of Sven and bent over to show her breasts to him. She pushed them in his face, and then busily kissed his head and neck. She brought her hands down to lift his tunic, but he roughly grabbed her wrists and stood up to face her. He looked straight into her eyes and said only, "No." He shifted his gaze back to the woman and began to sit down.

Freyja's face darkened. She felt anger well up inside her and she kicked the bench over just as he began to sit down.

She turned on her heel then heard Sven fall to the floor, but did not look behind her. Stepping through the doorway of the Mead House she lay back against the log wall. She bounced her back against the rough bark in agitation. Her shawl stuck on the bark, but she leaned forward and pulled it tightly around her shoulders. Her face twisted into a pout and her lips trembled, "Aaah, this is not right," she wailed.

She took a deep breath and mounted her horse to begin her solitary ride back to the farm. The forest rang with her fretful shouting, "Gods, I am for Sven. Sven is for me. Why is he not with me?"

This new feeling of jealousy filled her. Surely she had coveted things, like the wanting of her new shawl, but jealousy... involving Sven? She was for Sven. Sven was for her. It had always been so with all her people and the foretelling insured it.

She ranted her tortured laments at the night sky. Her face felt flushed and her voice shook as she continued, "How can the prophecy be fulfilled if we are not together? What is happening? What does this mean?"

Chapter Two

By the time she reached the farm she was emotionally exhausted, but felt strangely relieved. She put the horse in the barn and plodded to her bed. She threw herself on the bed with a puzzled frown and burrowed into the furs. Rest was welcomed by her weary mind and she fell into a fitful sleep.

Freyja woke late, still weary and groggy. She stretched her stiff body which did not feel rested at all. She opened her shuttered window to find the horse outside it. Arndis must have let him out of the barn. He whinnied in greeting and brought his muzzle to her hand. "Oh, faithful friend," she spoke softly to the old mount, stroking his soft head.

"Freyja," her mother sang from the yard. "I hope you slept well, among other things," her grin from ear to ear. Freyja frowned. Memories of the night before rushed back and unbidden tears streamed down her face. Sobs wracked her body. Arndis' smile faded and she dropped the roots she carried as she rushed toward the house.

Arndis entered the room to find Freyja back on the bed in tears. "What is it? Where is Sven? Has he succumbed to some wound? Is all well with his parents? Was there a fight?" Arndis' questions came one after the other which was just as well since Freyja could not speak. Arndis sat down on the bed and gathered her daughter in her arms, "Tell me of your tears." As she waited for Freyja's sobs to subside, she fingered the necklace the young woman wore. The only thing they had of Freyja's father. Her own face reflected her daughter's pain.

"Mother, Sven would not come with me. He said, no! He would stay to do his captain's bidding rather than come to my bed. It is not right. How will the prophecy unfold? Why is he not here? What is wrong with me? Why does he not want to be with me?" Freyja dissolved again into tears.

"Hush now, shhh," Arndis patted her daughter and rocked her. "Perhaps there are things about their voyage we do not know. His captain must have a good reason for Sven to stay in the village. It is nothing against you."

"But," Freyja fumed, "Sven said, No, to me. He has changed. Some illness of his mind has taken away his good sense. He does not remember the prophecy and what we must do."

Arndis smiled slightly, "Freyja, it is your young mind with illness. You must believe in the prophecy, just as I believe that the coin your father left in remembrance will one day bring him back into our lives. You know nothing of the captain's order and are making too much of this. How did Sven greet you at the ship? I saw you together at the Mead House and he was in fine spirits."

Freyja sat up and wiped her eyes and a slow smile spread across her face. "At the ship he was happy to share my skirts. We knew each other well."

"Freyja, at the ship?" Arndis asked with a surprised gasp.

"Well, no one was around ...well, hardly anyone ...just a few people." Freyja's eyes twinkled deviously.

Arndis' eyebrows lifted. "Oh. Well then, you see, all is fine. You two seemed quite happy at the Mead House, too."

Freyja's face darkened, "When I wanted him to come to my bed he said, no. He looked at the black-haired women and said he must watch them for the captain."

"Oh, Freyja, you make too much of this and will find the truth when you go to the village. You will see." Arndis stood up to leave and kissed Freyja on the top of her head. She laughed quietly and mumbled something to herself as she left the room, shaking her head.

Freyja's whole demeanor changed as she jumped up to busy herself for the trip to the village. She washed her face and combed her hair. She ate what she could find quickly and grabbed some trade items, just in case. A skin for sleeping (she thought hopefully) and her new shawl for the chill evening were hurriedly tied in a bundle. The horse seemed eager to be ridden so they soon started off.

As the horse passed the meadow, Freyja thought to stop at her altar grotto. She slipped lightly from the horse and fairly danced to the secret ledge. Then she came to a stop mid-step with a troubled look on her face. The grasses with which she had bound the carved Sven and Freyja stones together had withered. The woven fibers of the dry grasses had pulled apart, unraveling the bond of the two statues. The two figures had come apart and a black stone had fallen between them.

Freyja had visited her altar often while Sven had been away on the viking. This figurative uncoupling was unsettling.

Freyja's hands shook slightly as she stood the figures up, side by side. The black stone, she brushed thoughtlessly to the side. A worried look came over her face and she touched the coin around her neck nervously. She stood silently for many minutes.

Then, at her altar, she felt the inspiration of the gods. She was warmed with the light from *Sol* as the clouds parted. Warm rays caressed her and she felt empowered with renewed purpose. She stood tall and resolute, her shoulders back and chin held high, to make her vow. Loudly she proclaimed to the gods, "I, Freyja, promise to fulfill the prophecy for my people." She held both hands toward the sky, "I will make Sven love me. I will bring children forth." She placed greenery and stones at the feet of the two carvings. "Our village will have the good fortune to trade with many and prosper greatly. With the gods help and guidance Sven and I will know the mighty passion, *inn matki munr.*"

Chapter Three

The next morning, Sven was assigned to sit beside a small fire. Above him, on a slight rise, was a tent which now housed the black-haired daughter of an Irish chief and her maid servant. He sighed realizing that this day would most likely be too long and too uneventful.

As he sat, guarding the black-haired woman, Sven thought of Freyja. Yes, she was beautiful. Yes, she was strong and capable. Yes, her body made him feel much pleasure, but he did not feel love for her like those who wrote the *mansongr,* or maiden-song poems, for their lovers. When Freyja had attempted to corner him at his post at the Mead House, he had to push her out of his mind and also physically away to continue his mission. For this his seat had disappeared and he tumbled to the floor, a victim of Freyja's jealous mischief.

He poked the fire now and again and let the flames mesmerize him. He wondered about the state of the family farm. He thought of home, which held little excitement compared to the excursion of late. He had seen new lands, fought for his friends' and his own life, and returned changed. Although he longed for the peace of the farm, there was still a part of him which would never again be satisfied with only farming. He would gladly board ship when the ice broke again in the spring. The fire burned low, coals putting forth a pervasive heat and a deep red-orange glow. It would be well that he follow in the footsteps of his father and his fathers before him; to farm and viking in their own seasons.

Freyja reached the village on the old horse just as the sun began to set. Her day had been beset with myriad emotions. Morning had brought tears when she remembered Sven's rejection at the Mead House the night before. Her mother's soft reassurances had soothed her and given her hope. Her plea to the gods must have been heard as evidenced by the clouds parting and the midday sun pouring down upon her. She had been filled with an inner warmth and inspired to reclaim her rightful place in the village's future, next to Sven as the prophecy foretold.

"Karle, do you know where Sven is?" she asked the young man outside of the Mead House. He was a friend to Sven and well known to Freyja.

Karle motioned with his hands full of tools, "I left him by his fire. He is to guard Brigit."

Freyja continued in the direction he had pointed and found Sven sitting on a log by a small fire. "What do you do here?" Freyja asked as she snuggled next to him on the log. His body felt especially wonderful against hers and a warmth began to build where they touched. Sven explained that the captain had men erect a tent for the two captive women. "Then you must be tired. Let us go to the

Mead House and then to rest our tired bodies, together," she said pointedly. She placed her hand on his thigh.

Sven did not respond to her touch, but replied, "I must watch Brigit."

"Who is this Brigit?" demanded Freyja sourly.

Sven pointed toward the tent with his chin, still poking his stick at the fire. "The captain and the servant woman know each other's tongues and she told him that the girl's name is Brigit."

"Well, it seems that those two indeed know each other's' tongues," laughed Freyja as she pointed to the two of them wrapped in a passionate embrace up on the hillside. The captain and the woman began to wander toward the Mead House. "See, they know to go to the Mead House. No one will bother the girl, now come," Freyja pleaded while standing and pulling on Sven's arm.

Sven replied harshly, "I must stay Freyja."

"Then we will make good use of the fire and your log," she said with a devious twinkle in her eye.

She stood and lifted her skirts to face Sven and straddled his knees. Bent from the waist she kissed him deeply then thrust her ripe breasts into his face. He breathed in her womanly scents and buried his face between her full, round treasures. She was giddy as she reached to lift his tunic and find his offerings. He moaned with pleasure as she began to work his flesh. His face was turned from her as her eyes beheld the magic of his metamorphosis. Seeing that he was full and feeling her own yearnings, she lowered herself to engulf him. Pleasure shot through her as they fit together and moved to the rhythm of their needs. She buried her face in his neck as they worked out their love making to erupt in an explosion of pleasure. She shuddered against his body and unwrapped her arms from around him pulling away to look at his face. Her eyes sought his in an effort to share the fire she felt, but he did not return her gaze. He was looking away, up the hill.

Freyja looked over her shoulder to follow his gaze. Darkness had fallen and the tent on the rise was now aglow from the inside with candlelight. The shadow on the wall of the tent was the profile of an obviously female form. The silhouette had taken her hair loose and now shook it out. It cascaded down her back and curled about her knees. Her clothing must have been removed as Sven watched and now her breasts clearly became the focus of the shadow theater. Sven never took his eyes from the glowing apparition.

A dark rage boiled up within Freyja. Sven had not made love to her, but to the shadow on the tent. She slapped him and he looked bewildered. He reacted by pushing her off. They both stood, neither understanding what exactly had happened. "I must see the captain... Gunnar," stammered Sven as he rushed away. Freyja sat down heavily by the fire.

Moments later she was on the move; a mission unplanned, but fueled by the betrayal she felt deep within her. She crept to the door of the tent. The older woman had returned from the Mead House and was now helping Brigit into a tub. "So, they give the child a bathing," she smirked to herself. When the woman came near the door Freyja pulled her out pointing the knife she always carried in a menacing way. The woman's eyes widened and she ran toward the Mead House. Freyja slunk inside and approached the tub. "You are but a child, not near a woman," she hissed. "No man has kissed these lips and Sven will not." She grabbed the girl's face and leaned forward to put a rough kiss on the frightened girls' lips, then slapped her mouth. Brigit quickly raised her hand to her reddening mouth. "You have had no man between your thighs," Freyja spoke through clenched teeth and splashed the bath water high as she slapped at the girl's crotch. "You are not for Sven. I am for Sven and he is for me," Freyja snarled.

The girl was obviously confused and could not understand Freyja's words or her intent.

"Your breasts will not be for Sven. They have pleased no man. See they are but small...," Freyja grabbed a breast in each hand. "But... your neck has been caressed by a golden chain." She stopped her tirade. She had felt a trinket between Brigit's breasts and ripped the chain from around her neck.

"That is mine," shrieked Brigit, in her own tongue, as she grabbed for Freyja's hand and the necklace within it. Brigit sunk her teeth into Freyja's forearm as she pulled Freyja into the wooden tub. The two women flailed about. Freyja had broken the gold chain and now it along with the trinket that had been in her hand fell to the bottom of the tub, hidden by the frothy water. Brigit scooped her arm down to try to find it as she pushed her other hand into Freyja's face. Freyja then grabbed Brigit to try to force her head under the water. They battled back and forth. The crowded space had them struggling for the bauble until both were drenched head to toe and had somehow struggled to their feet in the tub.

Sven had heard the screaming and ran to the doorway of the tent to find the two women engaged in watery combat. He grabbed Freyja and lifted her out of the tub, placing her in the doorway. "Out," he shouted. "Go, now," and turned back into the tent.

His eyes fixed upon Brigit and he stared open mouthed for a long moment. Her body was strong, yet graceful. She seemed as fit as a Norse woman, but her hands were delicate. Perhaps they had seen little work. Her eyes were a bright blue framed with dark lashes and brows which made a stunning contrast. He felt as though he could not free his eyes from starring, as though bewitched by her beauty. Brigit stared back with open, honest eyes, head held high and unashamed.

The other woman bustled into the tent with the captain, Gunnar, following. She quickly tried to sooth the shaking girl with soft tones as she helped her out of the tub and wrapped her in a cloth. The two women began chattering wildly and the captain interjected periodically. "Sven, Sven...," Brigit repeated while the woman helped her into a gown.

Between the captain and the two women they figured out that Freyja had been there, talking about Sven. The captain laughed it off with a shake of his head, "Women," was all he said. He patted the servant woman on the butt and pulled her out of the tent, laughing.

    Sven turned to leave, but Brigit grabbed his hand. She stood upon the wet floor in her bare feet, with her bedraggled hair, and he could not resist her forlorn look. She shivered and he reached out to close the flap on the tent. On one side of the tent was a chest that had been brought from her home on the Far Isle with clothing spilling out of it. Directly across from the doorway was a pallet of skins for her servant, Nora, to sleep upon, where she also kept her pouches of herbs. On the opposite side of the chest was a low bench piled with skins.

    Brigit stepped around the tub, which took up the center of the tent, with tears in her eyes she patted these sleeping skins. She lay back upon her bed of skins while holding Sven's hand and he sat on the ground beside her. She whispered words he did not understand as she slipped into an exhausted sleep. Sven touched the soft skin of her hand within his with awe. He no longer felt that he had to protect this woman because of an order, but that there was nothing he would rather be doing. He brought her hand to his face and brushed it against his cheek. He breathed in its aroma and with an enchanted sigh, put his head upon her bed skins and closed his eyes.

Chapter Four

Outside, Freyja angrily stomped down to the log in front of Sven's fire and sat to dry herself. Cold water dripped from her clothes and warm water from her eyes. Her breath came loudly and quickly as she tried to calm herself. Sven must have been entranced by this black-haired woman. What powers did she possess? She opened her hand to see what magic amulet might be on the end of the golden chain.

Her free hand rose to her mouth as she gasped. Closing her hand around the necklace, she ran to her horse, jumped on his back, and rode quickly toward home and her mother. She did not slow to notice the numerous signs of the changing season. The birch trees were beginning to change into their yellow leaves, berries and mushrooms were abundant and easy to spot. Though the day's sun had felt warm, the evening air was now crisp. Noticing such things would have taken her focus. Her only goal was to assuage the mixture of confusion and fear rising in her chest.

Freyja dismounted without dealing with the horse and ran into the house. She slammed something on the table beneath her palm and yelled at her mother, "Tell me!" She peeled her hand away.

Arndis turned from the fire she was tending. With a start she noticed what Freyja's hand had uncovered. She looked on the table and stammered, "How... What... Where did you...?" She sank down upon a bench as tears filled her eyes. There on the table were two halves of the same coin. One on a golden chain, the other on a leather thong.

"This must be Brion's coin, but how...?" began Arndis.

"Tell me Mother," said Freyja between clenched teeth. "What is this, I see?"

"This is the remembrance that your father and I made on a night such as this, long ago," Arndis smiled between her tears. "We knew we had very little time left together."

"Everyone had gone to the Mead House to celebrate the return of the ransom ship from the Far Isle. Og's father was Headman at the time and took the ransom in, saying that it would pay for all celebration of the night. Later the treasure would be divided by the families after the Headman took a cut for his troubles. My parents were sure to spend the night there. I came home quickly to tell your father that he would leave with the next high tide to return to his people. We cried and held each other, then decided upon a remembrance as a pledge of togetherness. We sharpened my father's axe and heated it in the fire. Then we cut a coin into two halves."

Arndis pushed the table leg aside, revealing a black scar on the plank floor. "We then made the holes by heating a nail and melting a hole in each coin half." She showed Freyja some marks on the floor near the hearth.

"We put each half on a leather thong. We went to my sleeping platform and made love, cried, and slept in each other's arms until dawn. By midday, my parents came home and Brion was taken to the village to be sent back to his people."

Arndis smiled between her tears, "I wore my half coin around my wrist and then around my neck, as you do now. I never took it off until I gave it to you. It is all we have of your father and I thought you should have it." She paused and looked down at both halves, bewildered, "But how have you both of these?"

Freyja asked if Arndis had seen the dark-haired women the night before in the Mead House. "Yes, the girl and the woman. They sat by the fire with their cloaks over their heads."

"Sven has been tasked with guarding this girl, this Brigit, as we wait for ransom from her father in the Far Isle." Freyja's voice had taken on a bitter tone, she nearly spat the girl's name. "She was wearing this."

"And how did you come by it?" asked Arndis.

"I have taken it from her as she has taken the heart of my man," responded Freyja a bit too earnestly.

Arndis' eyebrows lifted, "Freyja, I know you not to be a thief. You must give it back to the girl and ask her how she got it. Perhaps she knows of your father, Brion."

Freyja stomped her foot, "Mother, do you not hear me? This girl has bewitched Sven. She may have also gotten this coin through her magic. She may have even killed my father," Freyja's voice rose in a dramatic high-pitched tone and she began to cry.

Arndis stood and gathered her in her arms, "Here now, sit and have some stew. We will talk more in the morning. You will feel better with a clear head, after a good night's sleep. I will go with you to the village to find out how this comes to be around the girl's neck." She stroked the coin with a finger as she guided Freyja down upon the bench.

Between mouthfuls of stew and tears Freyja managed to mutter, "The horse."

Arndis patted her back as she walked past, "Do not worry, I will care for him." She shook her head thinking Freyja was making too much of the captive girl and Sven.

She mused to herself while dealing with the horse, "Perhaps I may learn of Brion and how his coin came to the girl." Tomorrow could reveal long awaited news of him. She dared not dream what that could mean to her. She smiled as memories of Brion flooded back.

When Arndis had learned that Brion was to be returned to his home in Ireland the next day, she was heartbroken. She went reluctantly with her parents to the Mead House. When urged to take another cup, she sighed deeply telling her parents that she was ill and would return to the farm early. She hurried from the Mead House and rode the horse hard in order to have the most time possible with Brion.

Arndis found him in the barn and ran into his warm, familiar arms, "You are to go to the village in the morning. This will be our last time together. Come." She took him by the hand to the wooden bathtub on the porch. She heated water on the fire and when the tub was filled, she slowly removed his worn clothing. Her hands were gentle as she helped him into the tub and washed him sweetly. Her hands caressed each muscle as they slipped smoothly over his skin. When she had washed his hair, she took her own clothes off and stepped into the tub with him. She stood facing him with no shame, presenting her body as a treasure. His face was soft with reverent awe and he smiled upon her. He held his hands out to her to help her settle into the tub.

Arndis lowered herself slowly into the wooden tub and water sloshed seductively over the top. Her thumbs gripped on to the wood grain on the inside that was raised by the use of water each Saturday. Her fingers felt the warm wood and lightly touched the cooler metal band on the outside of the tub. She let her shoulders relax as her arms entered the warm water. Her skin tingled with possibilities.

Brion washed her body with care, letting the water he cupped in his hands fall slowly over her shoulders. The warm water cascaded down her beautiful breasts and she closed her eyes with pleasure. When they were both clean, Arndis stood and helped Brion stand. They had relaxed in the warm water and then went to the fire to dry where Arndis had laid soft skins.

"Have you a coin, Arndis? I will make a remembrance of this night and our love for each of us to carry," Brion spoke excitedly. Arndis found a penny in her pouch.

"I see what you do," Arndis said with excitement as she helped make the mementos. She ran to get a piece of leather thong for each of them. Brion took one and tied it around Arndis' wrist.

Arndis took the other and tied it around his wrist saying, "We declare ourselves Brion and Arndis bonded and with taking hold of hands observe the pact between us." It was in this manner, they made their *handsal*. She knew it was not legal nor witnessed, but felt that her heart, like the half coin, was now tied to Brion.

They joined hands then fell into each other's arms. Arndis started to pull Brion to her bed, but he pointed his chin toward their tools, left out. Arndis laughed as she scooped up the axe, nail, and leather. The items were quickly returned to their places. She winked as she pulled on Brion's arm again, but stopped to pull the table leg just on top of the spot on the floor that had been cut and scorched by the hot axe. Brion teased her, not moving from the fire, then ran ahead of her to the bed.

They found each other under the furs. Clean cool skin touching. They warmed quickly as their passion ignited. Arndis straddled Brion to kiss down the length of his body, from mouth to belly. His fingers played in her hair as her mouth titillated him. When he was fully aroused, she stalked her way up and on top of him to satisfy them both. Brion took his turn to adore each part of Arndis' body and pleasured her tremendously. They lay in each other's' arms until they heard Arndis' parents on the road. Their goodbye kisses were long and tender before Brion left through the window, slid to the ground, and ran to the barn.

Chapter Five

When Freyja awoke, her mother was already busying herself to go to the village. Her basket was packed with rabbit pelts and roots and she smiled widely as Freyja approached the fire.

"Today we learn of Brion's coin," Arndis fairly sang.

Freyja scowled and her mouth twisted, "I do not want to talk to the girl. She may bewitch us all as she has done to Sven. *You* can speak with her."

"Freyja, you must give back her necklace and we will ask her the story of it." Arndis sighed slowly and patiently. "Now ready yourself. We go," was her stern finish.

Freyja seemed to drag her feet, but her mother kept pushing. She even put the new shawl around Freyja's shoulders, though the girl seemed unenthusiastic. Freyja had eyed the beautiful *nalbinding* shawl, made with woolen thread and one needle, by the twins' mother of the neighboring farm for many market days. The twin girls had modeled it on each occasion and Freyja wished mightily for it to be on her shoulders, under Sven's arms. When she finally had enough to trade for it, she was ecstatic. Now it brought her no joy.

When finally ready, they walked to the village. Arndis hummed and swung her basket. Freyja kept her answers clipped when her mother would mention something she noticed or tried to make small talk. The girl, who always found something in the woods to enjoy, found nothing to lift the corners of her mouth. She was thinking only of the look she had seen on Sven's face as he watched the shadows debaucherously cast on the wall of the tent. *How could he stop loving her?* The time away on the viking and this wicked girl had changed him.

Arriving at the village Arndis looked a question at Freyja. Freyja pointed with her chin and Arndis and Freyja walked around the corner of the Mead House. Sven was again seated at his fire. Freyja stepped toward him with open arms, ready for an embrace. He looked up to the tent and swallowed hard. Sven did not stand in greeting as he normally would and only nodded at both women.

Arndis broke the tension, "We go to speak to the captive girl. I hear Gunnar knows her language. Bring him to us." Sven frowned but stood and left to retrieve his captain. Freyja stared after him with an open mouth until her mother pulled on her sleeve and nodded up the rise at the tent.

When they came to the opening of the tent Brigit stood and started yelling at Freyja who tightened her jaw and clenched her fists. The servant woman and Arndis both stepped between the girls. They were trying to calm each of their charges when Gunnar entered.

"Peace women," he said, "These women have come to speak with Brigit," he spoke to the servant woman, "I will help as I can," he winked at her.

Arndis knelt on the ground and patted it while looking at Brigit. Brigit and Freyja sat down opposite each other, glaring as they did so. Arndis spread out a rabbit pelt in the center of the women and reached into her basket. When she held up the coin on the gold chain Brigit reached out to grab it, but was stopped by Arndis' stern look and firm, "No."

The coin was placed in front of Brigit on the rabbit skin and then Arndis placed the other coin in front of Freyja. She pointed to the gold chain and then to Brigit and then pointed to the leather thong and to Freyja. Brigit's brows knitted and she looked a question at Freyja. Arndis seemed to understand and looking at Gunnar said, "Tell her that this half-coin first belonged to me and then I gave it to my daughter." Gunnar relayed the message to Brigit adding that the first owner of the coin had been Arndis.

"Arndis!" the girl spoke with surprise and excitement. She grabbed for Arndis' hand and began to babble. Gunnar could barely keep up as Brigit told her story.

"You are Arndis?" Brigit asked, "My father, Brion, has spoken this name many times," translated Gunnar. With a gasp, Arndis squeezed the girl's hand. "He told of your caring for goats and trapping of rabbits together. He spoke of your eyes and your laughter as you worked in the barn and how he fell in love with you in the time of his capture." Arndis let go of Brigit's hand and her head rocked back as she both laughed and cried. A wave of emotion hit her after years of worry and wonder. *Brion had lived to have this daughter!* Then Arndis thought of her own daughter. Daughter of the same father. *What must she feel at this moment?* She looked with shining eyes at Freyja.

Freyja sat with a scowl on her face and an open mouth, her eyes moved back and forth between her mother and her... SISTER? The thought was shocking and unwelcome. Her breath came fast and hard as her head swooned. The realization was too much to take in. She stood quickly, as her jaw clenched. She turned to run out of the tent, then everything went dark.

Chapter Six

Freyja heard voices as if they were far away. Her eyelids fluttered. She felt warm and comfortable on a soft skin and let herself fall back into an emotionally exhausted sleep. Arndis stroked her daughter's hair as she talked softly with the other daughter of Brion. They had put Freyja on Brigit's sleeping platform when she fainted and now spoke in low tones as they watched her.

"She has had much on her mind lately," Arndis nodded toward Freyja. Gunnar continued to translate. "Since the men retuned from the viking, with you, her lover has been a changed man. They have been as much as promised to each other since very young and now he may be pulling against the prophecy of their love and life together. For the good of the village, they must have children. They will fulfill the prophecy and bring prosperity to our village."

"I understand," said Brigit, "Our clan also had a prophecy about my father. It was told that his heirs would bring prosperity and we are still waiting."

"Yes," replied Arndis, "a prophecy always seems to keep the people waiting. We ask often, when will we see it? Perhaps we should ask the Old One of our village. It is she who cast the runes and first read the prophecy. Yes, this is a good thought. Freyja is a favorite of the Old One. She will tell her all that she knows and sees."

Brigit reached out to lift her half coin on the gold chain. She smiled as she looked at Arndis. "My father loved you very much and spoke of the night you made this. He gave it to me when I became a woman. He said he hoped that it would lead me to such a great love." She picked it up and placed it around her neck as her eyes met Arndis'. Arndis nodded her approval.

"And your mother? Did he not love her?" Arndis was not sure why she asked. Time and distance had surely changed Brion. She blushed with embarrassment at her questions.

"My parents had an arranged marriage, between two clans, to strengthen trade and defense against the Norsemen," she glanced quickly at Arndis. "They became great friends, but had no passion. My father told me this. We were very close. It was also in hopes of fulfilling our prophecy as his offspring were to bring power and prosperity to both clans."

The captain stood and shook out his legs. "I tire of this woman's talk, though I never tire of women," he laughed as he pulled Brigit's servant to her feet and threw his arms around her, "We go to the Mead House for more entertaining talk." Gunnar lifted the woman up and carried her out of the tent as she giggled girlishly.

The noise roused Freyja and she sat up, blinking her eyes. She rubbed the back of her hand across her face remembering her surroundings. She slid off the sleeping platform onto the floor. Her eyes focused on her half coin necklace and she reached out to grab it as she crawled her way to the doorway.

"I am going home," she spat at Arndis and Brigit while finding her footing and stepping out of the tent.

Arndis' eyes followed her daughter. She sighed as she stood. Brigit stood as well and opened her arms to embrace the older woman. The hug felt very natural to both and they parted with a silent smile.

Arndis had every intention of walking home. She took note of Sven sitting solemnly at the bottom of the rise (still at his post to ensure the safety of Brigit). As she passed the Mead House, she heard some friends call out to her. *Perhaps Freyja just needed some time alone,* Arndis thought as she decided she might as well enjoy the company of friends before she began the trek that would end the long day.

Arndis walked through the door and almost ran into Helga dragging Og out of the Mead House.

"Arndis, we have been speaking of you," Og smiled and Helga made a disdainful face, "We need a place for the girl and woman from the Far Isle to stay for the winter. Your farm has done this before and you only have two mouths to feed now. The elders and I think you should take them."

Arndis could only manage a surprised, "Oh," before Helga pulled Og past her and out the door. Arndis looked after them with an open mouth.

"They will speak to her, Og. You are needed on your farm," Helga grumbled, glowering at Arndis.

Halig, the owner of the Mead House, pushed a cup of mead into Arndis' hand saying, "You are bold to take the captives in. They are to be guarded and protected, both. You will need your drink and are always welcome here."

Arndis replied, "Thank you?"

Others stepped forward to clap her on the back and buy her cups as she sat at a table. There was talk of wrapping up the harvest now that men had returned from the viking. There would be feasts in celebration of a good harvest and work to be done in preparation for winter. At the table of old men, many such men were volunteering to help as it insured them good food and time with families which they themselves no longer had.

Arndis, warmed by the mead and friends around her, thought more of the idea of having the captive women on her farm. Brigit and she had a burgeoning bond and her handmaid, called Nora, was quite pleasant.

"I thank you for the drink. We will see what the winter brings with two more women on our farm. Good night," Arndis said to her table of friends.

Stepping outside, she was glad of the cool breeze. It brought the forest into focus and hurried her steps. She was happy to soon snuggle into her bed for a restful night's sleep.

Chapter Seven

Freyja woke to the voices of women in the kitchen, chattering. She did not recognize the voices, nor even all the words and came out of her room with many questions. There seated at the table were Brigit and her servant.

"Ah, my dearest," Arndis cooed. "There was much talk at the Mead House last night and we discussed the coming winter. It was decided that Brigit and Nora," she pointed at the dark-haired girl and the servant woman in turn, "will stay at our farm for the winter. A tent is not fit for the weather and, after all, since Brion stayed here it just seems fitting." Arndis' voice sounded a little too bright. "Sven brought them early."

Freyja swallowed hard and looked around in anticipation. "He had to go back to help with his farm," Arndis continued. "Now, I can sleep with you and Brigit and Nora can have my room, unless you girls want to sleep together."

Freyja snorted at the thought and pushed past her mother to get some bread and butter. She stood while she ate. Arndis continued, "Brigit will come with us to the village. The Old One wants her to be at the Mead House tonight to cast the runes anew about the prophecy. Some are wondering."

"Wondering what?" shouted Freya with a mouthful of bread. "Have the daughters of Brion been confused? The prophecy is not about her. It is about me and Sven. Why WE were spared. What WE shall bring to the future." She stopped her shouting. Could this even be a question? What had Brigit to do with any of the prophecy? She grabbed her shawl from a peg and walked out the door.

"We *will* meet at the Mead House at sundown to hear from the Old One," Arndis yelled after her. Freya waved back at the house with one arm without even looking.

The bread in her mouth tasted dry and the butter did not help. She stopped at the well to get a drink of water. The familiar action of drawing the bucket up, with its sweet offerings, calmed her and she took a long drink from the wooden rim. The cold clear water overwhelmed her lips and ran down her chin until she lifted the bucket away. Wiping her chin and mouth with her arm, she felt satisfied and began to walk. She did not know where her feet were taking her. She soon found herself in her own sacred meadow and let the tears flow.

Freyja sat on a low stump and thought about the last days. Her love, Sven, had given her his passion seed while looking upon the visage of another woman. She had found that the only legacy of her father had also been left to a half-sister whom she had only just met. Now, that half-sister was to live under her roof at the invitation of her own mother! And now, the prophecy that had been her only claim to individuality and a future, was to be reexamined in front of the whole village! It was more than she was able to take in gracefully at the moment and she slumped from the stump, down on the ground.

She grabbed the brown dirt between her fingers and called upon the golden-haired earth goddess, Sif. "Sif, I call upon you to guide me." Surely, this goddess as well as the goddess for whom Freyja was named could put things right and return Sven to her arms, his rightful place, to fulfill the prophecy.

She sat on the earth which was barely holding on to the last of the summer's warmth and received the message more plainly delivered than she thought possible. *As the grains which grow upon a single stalk are separate from each other, so you are independent from Sven.*

Her brows furrowed, but her shoulders relaxed. She had been delivered a message, but what was she to do with it? She had been leaning against a stump and when she stood a thread of her shawl caught on the bark. One long thread pulled out across the width of her shawl. She wrapped it around her shoulders as she approached her altar to check on the carved stone figures of herself and Sven. The last time she had checked, she had left them standing side by side as she hoped they would in real life. She brushed away some twigs to find only the figure of herself and could not find the Sven figure, though she looked everywhere.

She began to walk aimlessly. Nature soothed her as her nostrils flared. The air smelled of an end to the summer rain, rich soil, and fall changes. The fresh breeze also made music among the tree branches to enchant her ears. She picked a stalk of grass to chew upon and stopped on the bank of the creek. The water was low at this time of year and she put her sturdy feet in the mud and squished her short toes. She looked around realizing where she had wandered. This was where she often washed clothes and where she and Sven had a love encounter.

She thought back on that day when she had felt so fulfilled. She remembered how Sven had lifted her skirts from behind and how he felt against her buttocks. Warm skin had thrust against her own cool skin, a shudder of pleasure made her chest rise. She had given in to Sven against the warmth of the rock she leaned upon that day. "Such pleasure is proof of our bond," she spoke aloud as she lay back on the ground. She stifled a cry then took a deep breath. She watched the clouds as she tried to slow her breathing. It worked and she drifted off hearing her grandmother's voice, *"Perhaps the inn matki munr is to be found elsewhere?"*

Freyja brought herself back from her daydreams and memories. Fingers, toes, ahh, she was alert now and sat up. Her shawl stayed on the ground so she pulled it up as she stood. Several more threads stayed behind, on the ground, as she gathered it into her hands. She walked toward the farm and the mud fell off her toes with each step. It was soon completely washed off as the clouds burst open and she was caught in the downpour she had smelled earlier on the rise.

Chapter Eight

A drenched Freyja dragged herself up the steps wanting only the fire. She looked and listened carefully, but the house was empty. The three women must have already gone to the village. She sighed deeply with relief.

After the rain came down in droves a chill had clung to her. Kneeling at the hearth, her supple lips pursed as she blew the coals back to life, adding kindling and a bit of wood. She mindlessly removed wet clothes and held her hands over the fire to warm them. Her body was warming and drying, lifting her spirits. She took stock of her naked form. She was strong with muscled arms and legs. Her breasts were full and round and fit her stature of a medium framed woman. Her hips and buttocks round and firm. She decided that these gifts must have come from the goddess of sexuality, *Freyja*, for whom she was named. *Certainly, The Lady did not have problems with men*, she mused with a tinge of envy.

Warm and dry at last, Freyja dressed in fresh clothes and ate a bit of soup still warm by the fire. She was happy to be alone and not have to deal with Brigit, but knew that she would most likely see her soon at the Mead House. She was not sure why Arndis had wanted to bring the ebony haired girl with her. After all, she was but a child to Freyja and village issues had nothing to do with her.

Freyja took a deep breath and steeled herself for the evening. Stepping outside, she was glad to see that the rain had stopped and also that her shawl had dried enough to keep her shoulders warm.

The first steps felt difficult to take as she was anxious about the evening ahead. The whole village was sure to be there and she and Sven would be the topic of discussion. The runes were to be cast again and the Old One would reinterpret the sixteen-year-old prophecy; "When Freyja and Sven couple and children are born then we will trade with many and our village will prosper."

Enough of the people of the village had been expressing doubts about the prophecy or at least impatience at the timing of its fulfillment. When Freya was only two years old and Sven was one, there was a sickness which killed all the other children younger than two and many of the elders (including Freyja's grandmother). When they asked The Old One why this had happened, she said in her sing-song voice that the old always die to make room for the young. She said that the village was going through changes for the future. Mothers were tested with the loss of their children, but more would come and one day there would even be prosperity for the village because of the prophecy for Freyja and Sven.

Today everyone knew that "Freyja is for Sven" as they said, because it was known that they were of the prophecy. Now it was also known that they had been together, but there had been no marriage negotiations or talk of bride price or dowry. None of Sven's family or anyone in the village had taken on the role of fastnandi for Freyja's family, as she had no male in her family to be a negotiator for her marriage.

Freyja shook off these musings and held the thought of tonight as a reaffirmation of the prophecy. The Old One would tell everyone that the prophecy was true and they were to help Sven and Freyja make it a reality. Love and prosperity would come to all!

She shook her shoulders and arms, then her legs, to make these thoughts physical. Yes, the night would set things right. She smiled and picked up her pace.

She caught a glimpse of a flame. Someone was lighting a torch outside the Mead House as sunset approached. Her timing was perfect. She threw back her shoulders and held her head high as she passed through the doorway.

"She is here," exclaimed Arndis and a general murmur of excitement ensued. Apparently, many had arrived early in anticipation of the evening. The only sound of disappointment came from the Mead House owner, Halig, as he, "Titch, tiched," since he had been making a profit from the early arrivals.

The Old One turned to the doorway with her aged light blue eyes and smiled. "Yes, she is here. Come Freyja. Come

Sven. Come before me as you did so many years ago. We will cast the runes once more."

Freyja came toward the front of the Mead House to see that Sven was already there, as well as his parents, her mother and Brigit and Nora. The Old One had created her sacred space and had a fur set out, prepared for the casting of the runes. The Old One bent to throw the bones, grabbed hands with Sven and Freyja, and lowered her eyes. "Uuuum, you were chosen from the sickness to lead us forward to prosperity and trade. Yes, it is still true... but... ahhh, there is something dividing you, pushing you apart," and she let go of both of their hands to slump down on her knees to touch the runes. "You, Freyja," she grabbed Freyja's hand to pull herself up though her head stayed down. "You will bring our village prosperity. And you, Sven," she grabbed Sven's hand and brought up her head, "will bring us trade." She raised her head to look long and pointedly at Brigit and Nora. "It is clear now; the runes have spoken." She raised all their hands triumphantly, showing a strength much younger than her age.

"Ohhhh," an excited murmur ran through the crowd and people nodded to each other as if they understood. Others raised their eyebrows as if to say they agreed, although they were not sure that they understood. Backs were slapped and drinks were bought to toast the future. Even if it was not understood, people wanted to believe in good fortune.

As soon as Freyja's hand was loosed, she looked for Sven. "You see, all is well," she sang as she grabbed Sven around the waist. He turned and sharply thrust her arm off. "Did you not hear?" he asked. "It has changed. You are to bring prosperity, and I to bring trade. We are independent of each other." It was almost exactly what she had heard from the goddess, Sif. Sven then walked away, without a backward glance.

Freyja took a startled breath and looked for her mother. Arndis was sitting with Brigit and Nora. They were sharing mead and much laughter. It seemed odd that her mother had accepted change so quickly. She approached them. "I am going home."

"Oh, so soon? We have seen such a change of fate, but the Norns have often used strange threads in their weaving. We will celebrate this clarity from the Old One and then be home. Good-bye then," Arndis hugged her firmly. Freyja smiled weakly and turned on her heel to head out the doorway.

Once outside, Freyja leaned against the rough bark of the Mead House's outer wall. This evening had not soothed her at all. The prophecy had been turned on its ear. She and Sven had been divided. No more would she hear, "Freyja is for Sven." She had now lost her position of respect. And doubt, or at least uncertainty, had replaced her previous place of honor. How would she benefit the village? No one knew for certain. She bit her lower lip and exhaled vehemently. She bounced her back against the wall several times as she clenched her jaw and tears came to her eyes. She was anxious not knowing what the future would hold. What was she to do? She leaned forward and pealed her back from against the wall. Several strings of her shawl stuck against the bark and pulled out as she leaned forward. She felt the resistance and removed her shawl to find many holes now in her prized possession. It was unraveling in front of her eyes.

Her shawl, her life, the prophecy... unraveling. If she was not for Sven, then who? If their coming together and children from them were not to bring the future good, then what would? She would bring prosperity? How? The questions filled her mind and she had to move. She walked with her shawl hanging from her fist. One foot, then the other, she stomped along. Not knowing where she was going.

She found herself, again, in her meadow. She went to her altar and once more she saw the carved figure of herself, alone. All of the future she had imagined for herself was gone. She had no idea of what was to come. Her future was no longer determined. She was lost. How could she *alone* bring prosperity to the village?

Chapter Nine

The party continued while Freyja walked home alone. Arndis was eager to learn more of Brion and queried Brigit through Nora. "You said your father spoke often of me, then married your mother to bring two clans together. To be sure, when he left, he did not know of Freyja, but once home he had you and raised a family. How is he now? Does he still tell stories of his time with me?" Arndis knew that her questions were fishing for fond memories to be revisited in her heart, but could not help the connection she sought.

Brigit's eyes blinked and her nose reddened. "My father was mortally wounded more than a year ago after we were raided by Norsemen," she lowered her eyes. "He battled to keep his family safe, but later suffered and died."

"Oh," Arndis cried, as she raised her hand to her throat. "I am sorry for this loss. I had hoped that he lived and I might know more of him." Her eyebrows pinched and she reached out for Brigit's hand. They clutched hands and tears came to them both. Arndis thought of the beautiful young man she had loved and Brigit of the father who had reared her and loved her for so many years. Memories flowed as the mead flowed and perhaps the mead made the tears flow more easily, but the two women had created a new bond, holding hands as if mother and daughter.

Sven watched the women from across the room. He heard their laughter and could not help smiling. His eyes sought Brigit then fixed upon her, he moistened his lips. He could feel his heart beating as he was overwhelmed with a sensation that was entirely new to him. His cheeks burned and he held his breath. He could not think clearly and thought he was becoming sick. Dizzily he stood up to head outside. His feet moved forward, but his eyes stayed on her. His movements were jerky as he approached the doorway.

"Good night, Sven," Arndis called loudly after him. He turned and smiled weakly at her with an awkward wave of his hand.

"Ahh," sighed Nora and waved back. She had watched him daily as he guarded their tent and marveled at him when he had come to their aid after Freyja had attacked Brigit. She sighed wistfully for her youth, with a heave of her chest and a sidelong glance.

Brigit's heavily lashed blue eyes looked up slowly and locked with Sven's for a long moment. She drew in her breath as her chest tightened. Her eyes trailed after him as he passed through the doorway, with a hunger to see his beautiful form again.

"Oh," Arndis gulped guiltily. "I wonder how Freyja is doing? Her heart may be broken by the runes this night. She was to be for Sven these many years. Now he may be gone from her life. I did not think on this. Perhaps I should go now."

"We will go now, as well," said Nora. "It is time for sleep." No one mentioned the fact that they had to go with Arndis as she was now their guardian. The women gathered their things and left the Mead House to walk back to the farm. They walked in silence through the dark woods, but it was peaceful. This night had changed things for them all, even if they did not yet know it.

Chapter Ten

The next morning Freyja woke with a start. There was a warm body next to hers, but it was her mother's, snoring away after a long night. She lifted a bear skin to crawl out stealthily, but her mother yawned and smiled. "Oh, there you are my sweet," Arndis said. "What does this day hold for you?"

Freyja glowered, "I have no idea. I have no past and no future. I am alone, without Sven, and do not know how I am to bring prosperity to our village," Freyja fairly spat the words. She saw her shawl on the floor and kicked it into the corner.

"Oh," replied Arndis weakly. She did not know what to say. "You should take the day slowly and see what comes to you. Perhaps some time with your goddess may guide you." She went to the corner and shook out the shawl.

"Yes, the goddess of passion will guide a woman, who no man will have, to save her village," Freyja said sarcastically. For years, only Sven had support to be with Freyja as the prophecy said. Others had been told to avoid her, as she was off limits, and had married all the available girls. Now only the old widowers or young boys were available to marry her. *Of course, she could always take up her mother's profession*, she thought sarcastically. This was not fair!

She grumbled to herself while she dressed and glowered at her mother. "What has happened here?" Arndis asked as she held up the shawl.

"It has come apart."

"How?"

"It..., I..." Freyja could not finish.

"Well, I will keep it for you. You may be able to repair it," said Arndis smoothing the fibers while hanging it on a peg.

Freyja did not look at her mother, but went to eat something. She was glad no one else was awake to ask questions or imply that she had done something to ruin her life. She decided to care for the animals and then go to check her rabbit snares. Perhaps the routine would soothe her.

Freyja meandered through the woods while checking her snares. The first three were empty so she slowed down purposely to avoid going home. She said a quick, though fervent, prayer to honor *Freyja*, just in case her mother might be right. Then she picked some berries and ate, feeling the sun-warmed ground through her skirts as she sat cross-legged. The warmth felt good as the air was now cool.

She thought she heard a woman's laughter. Wonderful, now even the goddess was laughing at her. She stood and brushed herself off. She kept walking and found herself in a small clearing. There was Brigit, smoothing her hair.

Freyja's eyes narrowed. "Why?" asked Freyja.

"I walk," replied Brigit as best she could, with a shrug, in the language new to her. Freyja turned her back on Brigit and walked into the woods. Brigit followed. Freyja made a guttural noise in her throat and clenched her teeth. There was a large rabbit, caught in her next snare. Freyja knelt to release the rabbit and Brigit joined her. Freyja grabbed her knife from its scabbard and with a wicked smile thrust the hilt at Brigit. To her surprise, Brigit grabbed it and quickly dispatched the rabbit. Freyja could barely close her mouth, her eyes wide.

They continued to find a rabbit in each of the next three snares. With Brigit's help, it went more quickly than ever and when they arrived back at the farm Brigit skinned all the rabbits. Freyja took the rabbits into the kitchen where she showed Brigit how to butcher them for a stew. Brigit smiled and followed Freyja's every move. This was new and she was truly interested.

Brigit pointed to Freyja's knife and the rabbits, then she pantomimed shooting a bow with a question on her face. Freyja understood and shook her head, no. She had never had or even used a bow. Without a father or a man on the farm, she had never been taught the skills of hunting or of warfare.

Brigit found Nora who then sat at the table with them and explained that Brigit had been taught, alongside her younger brother, many of the skills of hunting and warfare. "Her father indulged her because she followed her brother everywhere. She often seemed more boy than girl, when she was small. They tried to teach her the ways of the kitchen, but she would not stay as her brother was not there." Freyja's eyes widened, amazed. She had always wanted such training as a shield-maiden. But she had been denied, just like she had been denied so many things in life without a father. Brigit, on the other hand, had had the father that she was denied! Their father! Freyja knew the feeling of jealousy deep within her. It filled her with an awful pressure in her chest. She started breathing hard, eyes stinging, jaw clenched, then she slowly stood and turned her back to them. Walking out without a word.

Freyja, daughter of Brion, had been left to fend for herself. She kicked at a chicken. Brigit, daughter of Brion, had been taught and coddled with a life of privilege.

She picked up a stone and hurled it into the woods. It was not fair! Everyone had always known that *she* was chosen to bring forth the prophecy. Now she had nothing, no way to bring prosperity to the village. She plopped down on the ground and pounded it with her fists.

These new feelings had pulled her down, not just to the ground, but down from the high position that she had once held. Her face heated with anger at her father and mother. No, anger at her half-sister who had gotten what she herself deserved. No, anger at the Old One's readings. Her mind reeled with the feelings rising within.

She panicked and her hands rose to her throat and then her head. She grasped her hair between the fingers of her fists. She rocked back and forth wondering how she would survive living with Brigit. Then the thought hit her like lightening! Her hands and shoulders dropped. She sat up straight.

Freyja smiled slowly. She did have something of value, her half-sister, Brigit. A great ransom could be negotiated and bring prosperity to the whole village! She would call for a meeting with the Headman Og and the Old One. All people would come to the Mead House and she would propose the idea. She would bring prosperity to her people.

Chapter Eleven

News traveled far over the next few days. Freyja had called for the whole village to meet with the Old One to take a step toward prosperity! It sounded promising to all. Everyone seemed to be there: young and old, infirm and able.

The Old One stood in front of them, then asked, "Why have I been called again? Why have the runes been questioned?" Freyja stepped close to face her. "I have called you to ask how I am to bring prosperity to the village." Freyja spoke loudly for all to hear.

"I hear you, child. What do you know? You would not call for me unless you had a thought or a sign."

"I have had a sign. Prosperity lies in something we have of value. My sister, she is of value to her clan. She will bring us prosperity," Freyja stated with a firm stance and a raised chin.

"Yes... we knew this when we took her from her home," said Gunnar. He stood and motioned to include all who had sailed.

"Then we should send a negotiator for her ransom before the winter locks our shores," thundered Freyja.

"Patience. This was always our plan, Freyja. Before we knew this one was your sister, we knew she was of value to her clan. We will send for her ransom in the spring," the Old One said patiently.

"I think Sven should go," said Freyja.

"No," the Old One closed her eyes. "Sven will stay here." She thrust Sven down forcefully on the bench next to Brigit. With a strong, dramatic voice she said slowly, "We will send our negotiators in the spring and they will return with our prosperity! All hail Freyja!" She raised a hand and then brought it down to caress Freyja's head.

The room erupted with sound. "Hail Freyja," everyone seemed to be saying. The Old One took Freyja by the hand and led her discretely outside. "Your sister will bring you more than prosperity. It is now your job to be open to her and all that you will gain from her. Take care that you do not ruin all our futures." She looked at Freyja with disappointment. "I have always known you were named for the goddess because of your loving nature. Do not disappoint the goddess or the village." She dropped Freyja's hand and went back inside.

"So, my idea was not new, but at least it will begin in spring. I will be rid of this girl when the negotiator and the ransom arrive. Until then I will have to find a way to live with her," Freyja mumbled to herself. She smoothed her hair and skirts, then lifted her chin to join the village folk in the Mead House. All seemed to be in a good mood, with laughter and stories loudly being shared. She found her mother and Nora visiting with Gunnar and several friends and her eyes searched for Brigit. She was still sitting on the bench next to Sven. They were watching some others, but their hands were touching slightly on the bench. Freyja's lips pursed and her jaw set. She let out her breath slowly and sat down heavily.

"Mead," she sang, too cheerily. "Who has mead to share?" Og happened to be walking by and slipped his arm around her neck while thrusting a cup into her hand.

"I will gladly share with the woman to bring us prosperity. This is nothing new to me," he slurred close to her face. Freyja took his cup and drained it.

"Truly, you have shared much with many as a leader of our village. But some have also shared with you, hum?" She danced her fingers up his arm and with her other hand replaced the empty cup in his hand.

"What is this?" he blinked, wide eyed.

"It is a cup in need of filling," she cooed and smiled. He smiled in return with narrowed eyes as he wobbled off to get it filled by the exotic dark-haired beauty of the Mead House. Freyja moved on to visit with others before he came back.

Klause raised his cup, among others, when he saw her approach. "Hail Freyja, thank you for prosperity. No longer from your loins perhaps, but we will take it still." He grabbed her by the arm and pulled her down upon the bench beside him. "Here is to prosperity," he pushed his cup to her lips. She drank more than was necessary to fill the emptiness within her. There was talk and laughter and she heard none of it. She thanked Klause, giving him a kiss on the cheek and moved on.

She found her mother with Nora after several more such stops. Arndis was being treated by others as the "mother of prosperity." This had not happened since the prophecy was first told, so she was taking advantage of it. Mead was being shared and some promises of help until the negotiator of the ransom would arrive next summer. She was smiling, sleepily, and embraced Freyja. "My daughter, we are fortunate. We have buyers for some goats and help to dig next spring's garden. Now sit with us." Arndis pulled Freyja's hand to her cheek to rub it gently against her face.

They accepted more mead and good wishes until most everyone had gone home. "To bed, all," the Mead House owner shouted. "Out now." All who were left stood up slowly as they found their feet. Arndis, Freyja, and Nora linked arms and headed outside. In the fresh air they realized that they had forgotten Brigit.

"I will search for my charge," Nora volunteered and returned inside. She found Brigit and Sven still sitting side by side now clasping hands as they gazed into the fire. "Oh, come now," she implored of Brigit and pulled her up and then out the door.

The women stumbled slowly toward the farm with many stops to relieve themselves. They talked and laughed even though they did not always understand one another. When they arrived home, they wished each other a peaceful night's sleep and fell into their beds.

Chapter Twelve

Freyja's eyes would not open, though she could feel the sun upon her face. Warmth came in shafts through the open window. She heard voices in the kitchen and willed herself to sit up. Her movements were slow as she oriented her body. Her head ached and she remembered the night before. She ran to the window and leaned out, "Bleeck," she retched. Feeling a bit better, she stood up and dressed shakily.

Holding on to the wall, she made her way slowly to the kitchen to sit upon a bench. Nora took one look at her and handed her a cup of broth from the soup pot. Freyja mumbled her thanks gratefully, wrapping her hands around the warmth. Her mother gave her a knowing smile and a soft kiss upon her head. "You will feel fine soon. This is a special soup that Nora has prepared for just your ailment. It seems we are all in need of it." The three women sat in silence as they let the broth soothe them. After a time, Nora and Arndis began to craft some items from rabbit pelts while Freyja felt the pull of the outdoors. She took a second cup of broth with her to sit on the rock where she used to imagine herself a siren and often brushed her wet hair to dry in the sunshine. She closed her eyes as she tilted her face to the sun. It seemed so long ago that she had wished to sing Og to a watery grave, just as the sirens of song. She was glad that her mother no longer depended wholly on selling herself to make a living for them and that Og was no longer a frequent visitor. She sighed in remembrance of her own feelings of that time. Then she had looked forward to marriage and a family with Sven. Then she longed for his body to be close to hers and ached to be fulfilled by their lovemaking. She let out a long sigh. Many things had changed.

 She was no longer destined to be for Sven, Sven no longer destined to be for Freyja. She felt a twinge of longing as tears stung her eyes. Her heart still ached, but she was not sure if it was for Sven or for the way things had been. She had once had a future laid out for her and love guaranteed. She had a place in the hierarchy of the village to bring prosperity and good fortune. She had been foretold of children to brighten her future.

 Two little goat kids came to her and nibbled at her legs, making her laugh at their playful antics. She scratched their knobby heads and patted their little backs. They liked her attention until they heard their mother's "baa", at which they bounced noisily away.

 Her ears free of the goat bleating, she focused on a new sound. A low moan, almost like an animal in distress, caught her. She sat up straight and listened closely, to determine its location. It seemed to be coming from behind the barn. She put her cup down and gathered herself up to move toward the sound. It repeated as she moved toward it. When she rounded the corner, she found its source.

Brigit leaned back against the rough wood of the side of the barn with Sven pushed tightly upon her. The moans were coming from them as their bodies rubbed together. Sven hands were at Brigit's skirts and were lifting them. His face was nuzzled into her neck. Her eyes were closed and her face blissfully lifted.

Freyja reached for her knife with one hand and for Sven's hair with the other. She pulled with all her might. Sven tumbled backwards to the ground and Brigit stifled a scream as she ran off. Freyja knelt forcefully upon Sven's chest, grabbing his shoulders and shaking them. Her voice shook also, "So, this is what you wanted? A romp on a belly?" She slid her knees to the sides of his chest then lifted his tunic and her skirts, to rub her thighs against his chest. Freyja could feel him firm up under her and slid further down to his hips. She felt anger, and power. She grabbed his member and began to ...? What was she doing? She did not feel desire. She did not feel love. And in that instant, she knew she was no longer for Sven and he was certainly not for Freyja. She stood up, panting with anger. She smoothed her skirt to compose herself and turned her back on him. With a last surge of emotion, she turned violently around to face Sven where he lay on the ground and kicked him in the gut.

She stepped into the dark of the barn and felt a multitude of emotions flooding her as she threw herself down in the golden hay piled near the cow. She cried as she smiled.

She was happy she had disrupted whatever it was she had discovered. She felt liberated in some way, now that she no longer desired Sven. She no longer pined to belong with him in any way. She was proud, in some way, that she had saved Brigit from Sven as well. The young girl knew nothing of Northmen. Anyway, he was supposed to have sworn to protect her honor, not to take it. She stood up to embrace the cow, then planted a kiss upon its warm furry head.

She found Brigit by the well washing her face with the cold water. It was bright red and her eyes were swollen. Brigit turned away when she saw Freyja and ran into the woods. Freyja followed at a trot to catch up with the girl, cut her off, and grab her arm. They were near the meadow and Freyja steered Brigit toward her altar made of boulders.

She roughly positioned Brigit in front of the ledge and looked for her stones. She had carved stones as representations of herself and Sven. A black stone had recently appeared and she had accredited it to Brigit and her black hair. She found the Freyja stone on the ledge and scoured the grass to find the black stone. She pointed to the gray stone and to herself, then to the black stone and to Brigit as she placed the stone in her hands.

Clutching her stone to her breast, Freyja closed her eyes and lifted her face to the heavens beginning to invoke the goddess to come to her aid. She pleaded for guidance and some knowledge to be revealed to her as to how she should proceed in life. Time stood still and she felt a comforting presence. She was filled with calm and connected to some power, although not consciously aware of any message.

She opened her eyes to find Brigit on her knees with her stone in front of her. Her head was bowed and she too seemed to be asking for help from her gods or goddesses. Freyja sat on the ground and kept silent until Brigit opened her eyes. Their eyes met and at the same moment a small smile came to each of their lips.

Freyja rose and placed her stone on the altar then motioned for Brigit to do the same. The gray stone and black stone stood side by side. Freyja jerked her chin toward the farm urging Brigit forward. Following, she tripped over something. It was the Sven stone. She tossed it, unceremoniously, at the base of the altar. It (Sven) was no longer a part of her altar or her future.

Walking next to this girl, Freyja noticed that her jaw and fists were now unclenched. Her eyes took in the beauty around her. The trees were showing their fall colors and animals scurried for the nuts and berries to fill their larders for the coming winter. She was still not sure about sharing their home with these foreign women, but thinking about it, no longer made her chest tighten. She even smiled when she saw her mother trying to show Nora how to kill a chicken.

Nora was practically dancing on the stump as they watched the headless fowl do its last jerky movements. Arndis was doubled over, red faced. She could hardly see the bird through tears of laughter and made several tries to scoop it up into the pot of boiling water. She showed

Nora how to hold it by the feet to dunk it and after much encouragement got her to take over the job. Nora looked up proudly to see both girls hanging on to each other for support as their knees weakened with laughter. She stuck out her tongue then smiled broadly. The girls pulled their hands away hurriedly, without looking at one another, and rushed forward to busy themselves with helping.

    Brigit helped Nora pluck the chicken following instructions from Arndis while Freyja sharpened a knife. She made ready to butcher it and put it in the pot. The women decided to cook outside over the ready fire and enjoy the mild weather. "Perhaps we should ask Sven to join us?" mentioned Arndis in good humor.

    Freyja glowered with narrowed eyes and pursed lips. "Yes, perhaps we should call for Og to eat with us as well?" she answered with lips pulled back over gritted teeth. Arndis glanced quickly around as if she could find something to help her understand Freyja then quickly just shook her head and pretended to tend the fire.

    Freyja bit her tongue and left the three women laughing and cooking over the fire. She headed into the woods to check her snares. The first one was empty, so she reset and tested it as usual. The rest, as well, were empty. Odd that not one had caught a rabbit. Oh well, chicken was cooking and she would check the snares tomorrow.

Chapter Thirteen

After milking the cow in the morning, Freyja delivered the milk to her mother. Arndis would make cheese and use the whey to ferment some of the garden roots for the winter. She tended to the goats which also meant milking. (Brigit must be taught more of the chores, she thought, wiping a few sweaty hairs from her brow.) Eggs were collected and when she took them to the kitchen, she told Brigit to go to dig roots in the garden. The girl looked puzzled, but Freyja only pointed to her mother in hopes she would convey the message.

Freyja wanted to climb the rocky prominence to check on the restoration and winterization of their ship that would go to the Far Isle again. They would leave when the ice broke in early spring to negotiate for Brigit's ransom. After spending the time, to procure a negotiator, the crew would return to the village with the prosperity promised in the form of ransom. The treasure would bring the prosperity foretold and Freyja would then be rid of Brigit.

Climbing the rough boulders always brought back the memories of doing the same with her mother as a young child. They would watch the comings and goings of her grandfather's ships. The ships often left loaded with men and supplies and returned with fewer of both. It was part of life when raiding and exploring. On the other hand, the returning boats often rode low in the water, loaded with treasure and captives. Their lives ebbed and flowed with the seasons of raiding and trading and then the fall and winter.

Today Freyja could see men, like so many ants, scurrying about the ship. They would be repairing oars and oar locks and checking for any damage shipwide. Sails were already taken off the ship and being repaired. She thought back to last spring when Sven had gone on his first Viking. She had hoped that she might grow his child within her belly while he was gone; had hoped he would at least return to begin wedding negotiations and plan for their future.

Her face reddened when she remembered her greeting on his return. She had had a bold, fiery passion within her and kindled it behind a fallen tree on the beach. He had accepted her gladly, she had thought. Then the dark haired girl, in the black cloak, had stolen her future.

She saw the signal fire a few yards away and had an impulse to light it. Perhaps the gods, along with the nearby farmers and villagers, would come to her aid. No, her grandfather would never forgive her for using the fire so selfishly. Calling men away from their farms and leaving their own families undefended would be unforgivable to be sure. It had never been used, to her knowledge, and she took some time to build it up in case it ever was to be needed.

As she climbed down, she heard movements in the forest nearby. She could not decide what it was and moved toward the sound, away from the farm.

There was Brigit, obviously not digging roots. She had placed small pieces of wood on a stump and was throwing pebbles at them. Why was she playing when there was work to be done? This only proved that she was but a child. "Stop," yelled Freyja. "Get back to your chores." Brigit smiled and placed a rock inside a piece of leather and seemed to want Freyja to watch. She raised the leather piece, with the rock inside, and now Freyja could see that there were also long leather thongs attached to the piece. Brigit began to swing the thongs, leather and a rock rose high into the air above her head, in a repeating circle. At some point she let go of a thong and the rock flew, right at the bit of wood on the stump, knocking it off and to the ground. Brigit jumped up and down babbling happily at her accomplishment.

Now Freyja looked interested and approached the girl. She had seen some of the boys with slings before, but had never been able to look closely. Brigit eagerly opened the leather piece and showed the slits in the leather and how it would hold a rock. She slowly pantomimed the use of the sling. Freyja forgot that she was mad about the chores and stayed to watch the practice for quite a while. She left Brigit to her play, with a shake of her head, and walked back to the farm. A basketfull of recently dug roots had been left in the middle of the garden.

Freyja scooped up the basket and marched into the kitchen. She plunked the full basket upon the table with a loud thud which got the attention of both Arndis and Nora. "The girl is out playing in the woods and has left this in the garden." Nora shook her head, laughing.

Arndis surveyed the bounty, "It is good we have more to ferment for the winter. Freyja you will wash and cut them. I have whey coming off the cheese board now so it is good timing."

"Yes, good timing for me to work while Brigit plays," grumbled Freyja.

Nora chuckled, "She has always been good at choosing her own activities. The outdoors and the practice of the arts of hunting or war have always drawn her, more than the kitchen or the loom."

"She plays now with a sling in the woods and actually seems very good with it," Freyja acknowledged begrudgingly.

Brigit burst through the door babbling happily. Nora motioned to her to slow down and sit and she continued to speak hurriedly. "What is she going on about?" asked Freyja.

"She is getting better with her sling, but wants me to help her make a larger one which will be more powerful," explained Nora. "We have used your rabbit pelts that I have tanned, but may now look for other leather. Perhaps at the market gathering we will find something."

"There is no other reason you would want to go to the village?" asked Arndis with a twinkle in her eye and a sly smile. "*Eigi leyna augu ef ann kona manni.*" Eyes cannot hide a woman's love for a man," she quoted the saga. Nora blushed. "It is well that we all have love in our lives," said Arndis wistfully.

"It is well," interjected Freyja, "but apparently not true for ALL. I will take you to market."

Brigit was interested in the proceedings and asked Nora. "She wants to know if she can go with us?" Nora spoke. Freyja's eyebrows raised.

"I think it would be good for her to see more of our lands. Freyja, you can teach her more of our language as you show her," said Arndis.

"Mother, I do not want to take her." She had not had a sibling and now understood the feelings of an older sibling required to include a younger one. All three of the women smiled at her, encouraging her to make the magnanimous choice of including Brigit while Freyja looked from one to the others.

"I will get the horse," offered Arndis.

"I have herbs to put in a pouch I made of rabbit skin," added Nora. Brigit stood as if ready to go.

Freyja threw her hands in the air, "All right. She comes with us."

Freyja walked the horse, with Nora and Brigit, to market in the village. They passed the Mead House and joined the large crowd at the crossroads where the three roads met. Nora looked at every item spread on the ground or a bench and pursed her lips while feeling of each piece of leather or fur. She would place the piece between her thumb and forefinger and rub making a face of approval or disapproval. Finally, she settled on a small tanned doe skin. "Yes, this will do well. Do you have coin?" asked Nora of Freya. Freya nodded handing her a coin from her pouch. Then she looked around for Brigit.

She did not see her at first and a strange feeling of panic gripped her for just a second. Looking toward the path back to the village she picked Brigit out of the crowd. The girl had allowed herself to be swept along with the crowd walking the path to the Mead House. The panic quickly turned to disgust at herself, as she realized she had actually been worried about Brigit, then anger toward Brigit, as the girl had put herself in an unknown situation.

Freyja led the old horse and followed, with Nora, to the Mead House. She stopped the horse and noticed Brigit's dark cloak peaking around the corner of the building. Rounding the building she came face to face with Sven. He and Brigit were making moon faces at one another while holding hands. She roughly pulled Brigit's hand away. Her face darkened while saying to Sven, "No harm shall come to her." Sven's face fell and he looked sad as Freyja marched her charge into the Mead House and away from temptation.

Once seated, Freyja leaned both elbows on the table and gestured emphatically as she launched into a lecture about the captain's orders that no man should take advantage of her and that Sven could not be trusted. Brigit's eyes looked worried and nodded seriously, she seemed to follow the conversation. When she heard Sven's name her eyes brightened and she smiled.

"No," groaned Freyja, putting her head in her hands. Raising her eyes to meet Brigit's, she began slowly and pointedly, "No Sven. Sven is not for you. Sven is for…," her voice cracked and trailed off. She stopped and looked down at her hands. What could she say? There were no longer any guidelines. Perhaps she should just leave Brigit to her own devices.

At that moment, Nora walked into the Mead House. Freyja grabbed Brigit's hands and put them together, as if in prayer, patted them, and ran toward Nora. "I am done watching this child," she pointed at Brigit and walked away. She heard Nora's tongue start clicking as she bustled toward the girl. Nora sat and questioned Brigit for a quick moment then locked eyes with Gunnar. In short order, she stood and was drawn toward him as a bee to honey. Freyja just shook her head in wonder. It was as her mother had said, "Eyes cannot hide a woman's love for a man." Freyja wondered if she should have looked into Brigit's eyes.

She had no idea where to go, but decided on the table of the old men. They would tell good stories and soon tire, to leave their mead unattended.

"Freyja, welcome." "Join us." She sat heavily between two old warriors. "We are telling tales of valor, exploration, and of our friend's journeys to Valhalla."

"I am here to listen and learn," she said with a half-hearted smile.

She listened patiently and quietly for a time. Mead was indeed shared with her and she began to enjoy herself. There really were things to learn. These men had had experiences worthy of passing on and had many skills to share. Time passed and she realized she was surrounded by sleeping figures at her table and that most of the other people had left. She moved closer to the fire and curled up, much like one of her goddesses' large cats, making herself comfortable for the night.

Her eyes closed and she dozed off. Freyja had a recurring dream in which she was her namesake goddess. Sven had just entered her hall, *Sessrumnir*. She beckoned him, from her throne, to come to her feet and he obeyed. She descended and took his hand to lead him to her table. They ate a decadent feast then she roughly pushed aside the meal to try to pull Sven seductively upon the table. He resisted, so Freyja took his hand and led him to a massive and grandly soft bed. She lay back and opened her clothing, willing him to come to her. Her chest heaved with longing. He reached one hand forward, onto the bed, then kneeled and crawled forward, succumbing to her allure. Almost in her arms, he stopped and raised his head, as if hearing a call. He turned his back to her to sit on the edge of the bed as if in a dream.

Hundreds of silver coins sprang out of the floor of the hall as he watched. They began to sing and dance gayly. Freyja recognized them as children of Sven. They pulled on Sven's clothing and danced him toward a chest. He knelt and held the lid open to see it was filled with treasure. The children made a marvelous show of twirling and diving gracefully into the chest. Sven smiled at them and praised them greatly. When they had all entered the chest Sven closed the lid and stood. Without a backward glance at Freyja, Sven walked out of the hall, cradling the chest in his arms.

Chapter Fourteen

Freyja awoke with the morning sounds, drool on her chin and a sore neck from her awkward sleeping position. She felt disoriented by the dream. When she had it in the past, Sven and she had always shared passion before he left the hall. They had devoured the feast and each other. This time he did not share his body or his heart. He barely looked her in the eyes.

Freyja stretched stiffly and recalled her night. After relieving herself of her charge, it had been pleasant enough. She had learned even more of her village and her own grandparents. She now knew who had been the trades people and crafts men of the previous generations. Many who were now thought to be too old to participate still possessed valuable knowledge and opinions on who was worthy to receive that knowledge. The brothers, Hallr and Kofri, had learned the forge from their father's father. They made armor and swords and worked all metals. They were sure to have gone home, but she would speak to them again soon.

A young woman cleaning up, offered her some bread and broth from her rough but delicately shaped hands. The hair that peaked out from her head scarf was black and curly and her oval eyes crinkled as she smiled shyly. When she bent her head, Freyja saw a glint and realized she wore a jewel in her nose. She knew the Mead House owner, Halig, had slaves and wondered where this shy beauty was from.

Freyja drank the broth and began to feel awkward as the woman's eyes never left her. She thanked her and took a small amount of bread to begin the ride home. Her horse, happily grazing outside the Mead House, whinnied in greeting. She was in no hurry to get home, so she let the horse take them slowly toward the farm.

There was a chill in the air which reminded her that they would need to gather and chop more wood for the fire. The sunlight's warmth seemed weak even though it was bright. She closed her eyes and turned her face up to the sun to take in *Sol's* blessings. She listened to the quiet of the green forest for a moment, until it was interrupted by singing. The horse took them around a bend and they came upon Nora, singing as she fairly danced along the path. She was swinging her arms and her feet were moving her along the path like a child taken up with a daydream. Her face was radiating with joy as she sang.

Freyja was entertained and called out, "What are you singing about, Nora? I do not know your words."

Nora turned and laughed with surprise. She switched to Freyja's language. "I sing of love in the mountains, this beautiful morning, Freyja."

"Well, I do not have to guess that you stayed the night in the village and that it was eventful," she replied with a wink. Nora just smiled and giggled happily. They walked for a while in happy silence, until Freyja remembered Brigit.

"Is Brigit ahead of you, on the path?" Freyja asked.

Nora looked behind quizzically and stopped in her tracks, "I thought she was with you." Their faces showed the shame of irresponsibility at the same time and they hurried their pace.

"We are nearer the farm than the village, so we shall go on," stated Freyja matter-of-factly.

Nora nodded with a worried look, "I am sure she is fine."

When the path brought them within sight of the farm, they saw Arndis in the garden, warmly wrapped and digging roots. Freyja yelled, "Where is Brigit?" Arndis must not have heard for she only stood to wave gaily at them, then turned back to her task.

When they got closer Freyja and Nora both asked the question again, their words tumbling over each other's. Arndis looked at them oddly. "I am not sure. She went off after she fed the goats and gathered eggs. And why do you not come home till morning? Hum?"

"I slept at the Mead House." Freyja winced as she stretched her neck. Both Arndis and Freyja looked at Nora with raised eyebrows.

"And I, I shall see what needs to be done," stammered Nora with too wide of a grin as she bustled into the house.

Freyja went to the well and splashed her face with the cold water. She felt revived and resolved to make the day fruitful. She cared for the horse and decided to check her rabbit snares as she had neglected them yesterday.

The first snare was empty. The next several showed signs of animals having been there, but were now empty as well. She was looking down for rabbit signs when she heard a low growl. Kneeling on one knee to look under a blue spruce branch her eyes met with those of a she-wolf. Her fangs were dripping with the deep red blood of a rabbit she had extracted from the snare. The wolf dropped the rabbit and looked up at Freyja readying to spring at her in defense of its food.

The wolfs teats hung down full, but her body was thin. She was hunting not only for herself, but her pups as well. Her eyes were fierce. She stepped over the rabbit and crouched ready to lunge at Freyja's neck.

Freyja felt the hair on the back of her neck stand up and sweat broke out under her arms. She readied herself to stand with an arm in front and across her throat as she reached for her knife. This wolf looked strong and determined to feed her offspring. Freyja began bouncing a bit to bring energy to her legs for standing up quickly. The wolf growled watching her bounce and seemed ready to counter her movements.

Suddenly the she-wolf yelped in pain and looked to its side. She bent her head to grab the rabbit in her mouth. It yelped again, around the mouthful, then backed off into the woods. Its eyes did not leave Freyja until it was swallowed safely by the dense green forest.

Freyja looked in the same direction the wolf had responded to and saw Brigit jumping up and down in triumph. One raised hand held her new sling and the other, several rocks. Freyja sat firmly on the ground. Never had she been so happy that Brigit played with leather and rocks. Brigit ran to her.

"Thank you. You shall teach me this?" Freyja asked Brigit. Brigit beamed.

Chapter Fifteen

The next morning the half-sisters did their chores then left the farm for the woods. Brigit brought all her slings and started Freyja with the smallest to begin perfecting the art. They set up twigs and clods of dirt as targets on stumps. At first, they seemed to defy Freyja and stayed still, mocking her.

When Freyja shook out her hands in disgust, at her lack of coordination, Brigit held them together. She took a rock and walked it toward a dirt clod. It seemed a pantomime that the goal was only to make contact and they would work on force later. Brigit could now understand much and was learning many words, but contact and force were not yet among them.

With coaching from Brigit, Freyja began to hit most of her targets. After several hours Freyja's arms and neck were sore from this unusual movement so she called for a break.

They walked back toward the farm and Freyja climbed the rocky prominence to take in the view. Brigit followed as if she naturally knew the place. Freyja pointed out the ship that had brought Brigit and noted that it would leave from that place in the spring to retrieve her ransom. A scowl crossed Brigit's face, for just a moment and Freyja wondered why that was so.

Freyja dressed the signal fire and when Brigit saw what she was doing, she too gathered more kindling to add to the fire. Freyja explained that it had not been used since she was a little girl, by pointing to herself and then holding her hand as for the height of a child. She acted out people running hoping that Brigit would understand that in time of need it would bring neighbors and villagers to their aid. Brigit laughed, but nodded that she understood.

They sat down to quietly watch the stark beauty of the beach from their vantage point and Brigit spoke. "You took my coin," she touched her necklace "and I felt hatred. Now, I must live on your farm."

Freyja thought about their first encounter with embarrassment. She looked away, at the water as she spoke. "I too felt hatred. I thought you had bewitched Sven." Freyja paused for a long moment. "I am sorry."

They looked at each other in silence then stood. Climbing down the rocky prominence, they saw a rider leaving the farm as they walked toward the house. They stopped at the well for water to drink and wash and the open door soon brought laughter to their ears.

Inside, Arndis and Nora, were laughing so hard tears were running down their faces. It seemed that the Old One had cast the runes to pick the crew that would return to Brigit's people and negotiate her ransom. The plan was that they would go in spring and return late summer with the ransom and Brigit's chaperone for her return trip to the Far

Isle. Nora was ecstatic that Gunnar would stay behind, but their laughter was because Og had been chosen to go. Talk of his experience, knowledge, and position had flattered him greatly, but when he was told that it earned him the right to join the voyage he stammered and tried to argue his way out of it. "I give up this honor to pass it to the young. How else will they gain experience and rise to their own positions of honor?" he had blurted while clinging to Helga. Gunnar had relayed the story to the women with much acting out of Og's panic when he came by the farm to tell Nora the good news. He left her with a passionate kiss and embrace.

"So, Gunnar stays and Og goes. I will not challenge the runes, but it makes me wonder at the gods' sense of humor," laughed Arndis.

Freyja wondered too. Although Og was sometimes a bother, she was worried how he might fare on a rough voyage and time away from home. "He will surely be in *Odin's* hands," she murmured while shaking her head.

Freyja's mother slipped an arm around her and nodded, "Yes, we will wish him well and send him on his voyage with supplies and good will."

"And my captain will stay here where I can look after him," Nora grinned. They all shook their heads at her and rolled their eyes.

"Yes, and we will look after you," Arndis laughed playfully pulling Nora's hair.

"Be nice or I may not share what he has brought," Nora pulled a drinking horn from under the table, took a draught, and passed it to Arndis. They all gathered around the table to begin a festive afternoon of singing and enjoying a meal together. Freyja smiled as she thought, *this must be what it is like to have a family.*

Chapter Sixteen

Some days later Freyja was gathering eggs, Brigit was milking the cow, Nora was working in the garden, and Arndis was by the fire when Gunnar rode into view with another man behind him. Nora quickly stood up and brushed herself off. She smiled brightly and waved vigorously to which Gunnar responded in kind. He slid off his mount and went quickly to grab Nora around the waist and place a kiss upon her mouth. She was happy to respond.

The other rider slid off the horse slowly and stiffly walked toward the door.

"Og," gasped Freyja, "why are you here?"

"Gunnar is working with me this day," said Og.

"So, why are you here on our farm?" replied Freyja impudently.

"I will go with the ship to get the ransom for your girl, here. I feel it best that I train to sharpen my skills for battle. We have chosen your farm as there is open and level ground," Og answered.

"And fewer witnesses," Freyja mumbled under her breath. "It makes sense," she spoke loudly.

Og continued his way toward the door. "Where do you go, Og?" Gunnar asked tersely.

"I will see if Arndis has food or other to share," he grinned and did a little shimmy.

Gunnar ran to block his path with outstretched arms. "We are here to train and have no time for such."

Arndis came down the steps to see what was going on and Og came toward her with open arms. She crossed her own arms barring her chest as Freyja explained why he was there.

Gunnar went back to his horse to retrieve two swords then told Og to follow him. They began slowly going over basic sword work. Brigit ran to finish the milking and then to take her bucket inside. Freyja finished gathering eggs and took them inside as well. The two of them then hurried outside to watch.

Brigit grabbed a branch off the ground and began to copy the work of the men. Freyja picked up a branch as well and realized that Brigit seemed to know what she was doing. Had their father taught Brigit the way of the sword as well as the sling? Once again, she was jealous of the time Brigit had known with their father. She hefted the branch and began to copy what Brigit was doing. Brigit noticed and turned to face her. With a nod, she began training Freyja as Gunnar worked with Og.

Og grunted as he was reminded of his skill long ago. He sweated as he stretched and strained to defend against Gunnar. He was no longer light on his feet and was tiring quickly. He held up his hand after some time and kneeled to take a break. Gunnar whirled about and stopped his sword inches from Og's neck.

"All right, my friend, we will stop for now." He looked at Freyja, "Will you fetch water for us?"

Gunnar asked so nicely that Freyja did not argue, but hurried to comply. She brought back the bucket and Og tipped it up to drink greedily from it. Gunnar tapped on the bottom of the tipped up bucket. "Hey, warriors share," he looked at Og with a scowl and held out his hand. Og pushed the bucket toward Gunnar with an outstretched arm and wiped his mouth with the other.

Gunnar took his drink then held out the bucket to Brigit. She was able to take a quick sip. "You know the sword?" he asked. He handed Brigit Og's sword and picked up his own. "Show me."

Brigit felt the weight of the sword and knew it was heavy for her, but tried to compensate. She held her own, blocking his blows and her size lent well to turning and ducking under his moves. He did not land a blow on her and stopped, impressed. "You need more practice. You may train with us."

"And I? I never had a father to teach me as she did." Freyja pointed her chin at Brigit. "May I not learn as well?"

Gunnar was taken aback by this emotional outburst. "Yes, you too may join us," he stammered.

Og chimed in, "You have had me in your life and I will teach you now."

Freyja rolled her eyes, then shook her head. She slowly smiled at Og and let her shoulders relax. "I will learn with you."

There were more rounds of sword play, with Og facing Brigit and Gunnar slowly introducing Freyja to the sword. Finally, Gunnar had the sisters face off using their branches. They were placed in a stance, sideways to each other, with their branch in one hand. When Gunnar gave the word, they hit out at each other. They were adept at dancing away from each other while still reaching out. This made their bellies wide open to the other.

Gunnar yelled out, "You will be gutted, like a pig, if you do not protect yourself. You cannot stay so open. Show your shoulder to the other." They were serious for a while, then as they hit each other's fingers bits of silly rage flared up.

They focused on hitting each other's sticks so hard that they were turned into splinters while they laughed and fell, exhausted, on the ground. Gunnar shook his head. "To the farm," he said. They gathered themselves, under the late day sun to walk back to the garden.

Og walked slowly and when they got to the farm, he pleaded with Arndis. "I will need to rest this night with you."

Arndis replied patiently, "There is no place for you here. You must go now."

"But I am sore and tired, I cannot walk to the village," whined Og.

"Freyja can take you back. You cannot stay," said Arndis, gently, but firmly.

Freyja looked at her mother, annoyed. On the other hand, she had not been to the village for several days. Her mother pressed some coins in her hand and nodded toward the horse and Og.

Freyja rode the horse with Og behind her and they slowly headed to the village and then to Og's home. Helga came to the door as Og stiffly slid from the horse. She glowered at Freyja then quickly went to help Og inside.

Freyja called out, "Tomorrow you must walk to train with Gunnar. He said it is part of your training."

Og smiled weakly as Helga began to question him. Gunnar had not said this, but Freya thought it was a good idea even though a little devious.

Freyja was shaking her head with a wry smile as she turned the horse and fingered the coins in the pouch tied at her waist. She stopped at the Mead House and entered to find the old men's table full of her friends. The olive-skinned slave girl with the oval eyes was sitting with them and was speaking another language to one of them. She quickly stood up as if reminded of her place when Freyja approached. She smiled with her head bowed. From beneath a fringe of sable lashes framing dark eyes she looked up at Freyja as she slid by.

Freyja was loudly welcomed by the old men. She responded by buying a round and began to ask about sword knowledge. The brothers, Hallr and Kofri, recalled the days of making swords with their father.

"We made many good swords then. Now we do mostly mending," Hallr said wistfully. Hallr's long white hair was tied back then tied again and again along its length. His blue eyes were surrounded by so many laugh lines that it looked like he had smiled often. Above his white beard he had the ruddy complexion of a man who saw the sun. His arms were still stocky from occasional work at the forge and his hands were calloused and gnarled.

Besides making weapons, they had done their share of using them on their vikings out into the world. They could tell Freyja stories, and they did.

"Can you show me?" Freya asked them.

"You want to learn the ways of the sword?" asked Kofri. Kofri also had muscular though aged arms. His blue eyes peeked out from under a shelf of bushy gray eyebrows and his long gray beard contrasted with his bald head.

"I do. I never had a father nor brother to teach me. No uncle or cousin lived to do so and my grandfather passed before I was old enough to learn," replied Freyja wistfully.

"Ah yes. Your grandfather would want you to know," said Hallr. The brothers looked at each other and said together enthusiastically, "A shield-maiden!"

There was toasting until their cups ran dry and Freyja bade them goodnight with a kiss on each withered cheek. She smiled thinking of this unlikely support for her study of the sword as she climbed up on the horse. *A shield-maiden,* she turned these words over with excitement! These old warriors knew much and they were willing to share their knowledge. She hummed to herself as she rode back to the farm, now wondering again if this was what family felt like.

She put the horse away and crept quietly up the steps to the dark house. Passing by the banked fire she saw a form and realized it was Brigit sleeping on a sheep skin. She went into her room and pulled a skin from the bed to drape around the girl. She slipped into bed next to her mother, and tucked her right wrist was between her knees, as it ached from the sword work she had done this day. Now to sleep and dream of warrior maidens.

Chapter Seventeen

Freyja woke up before her mother and found Brigit tending the fire. "Why did you sleep here?" Freyja asked as she hung the pot over the fire.

"The bed is full with Nora and Gunnar," she said raising her eyebrows. "Thank you for the fur," Brigit handed it to Freyja who nodded and put it under her knees. She stirred the pot thinking about last night.

"Did our father teach you to fight with the sword?"

Brigit sighed, "He did not like that I was always with my brother. He taught my brother and I watched. He taught sword and shield and sling. I would try it with my brother when my father was not there."

"Are there women warriors where you are from? In your clan or others?" Freyja wondered aloud.

"Some, but not too many. Why do you ask?" Brigit prodded.

Freyja said, "It is the same here. Some fight and travel while they are young. They end up in *Valhalla* or come back to village life. I know none who live near our village, but would like to know some. There are stories in the sagas," Freyja's voice trailed off wistfully.

"Gunnar says he will teach us. We shall learn. Now eat so we will have our strength," Brigit handed Freyja a bowl and they ate warm stew. Freyja was able only to eat a few mouthfuls when footfalls were heard on the steps. Og opened the door panting and stumbled toward the fire. Freyja helped him to a bench and brought him water.

He nodded toward the stew with a pitiful face. "Helga fed me only a little." Brigit got him some stew and he settled in happily. "I should eat before I train."

Gunnar appeared from behind the skin door and Og started. "Arndis is sharing herself again?" he seemed offended as he knew he had not been welcomed for some time.

"What is this?" Nora came up behind Gunnar and wrapped her arms around him, smiling at Og. Arndis came out of Freya's room at the same time and Og seemed to figure out the answer to his question.

"We have several warriors here it seems. We eat and go train," Og made sure to finish his stew even though Arndis was trying to hurry the men out.

"We must tend to the animals and our farm. We must not let them distract us," said Arndis with a pointed look at Nora. The women ate and ran to milk the cow and goats, gather eggs, and tend to the garden.

When they finished several hours later the girls ran to her, "We will take water to the men and then gather kindling for the fire." Freyja thought this would appease Arndis as she grabbed the full pail. She and Brigit ran to the training area together.

Nora was already there seated on the ground with her *nalbinding* in her lap. She was working on woolen caps to take to barter in the village and was thoroughly enjoying the entertainment. It truly was a sight. Gunnar looked good and was moving steadily. Og looked worn out and a little comical as he was still relatively uncoordinated. Gunnar would call out often, "Once again. Try to move smoothly as you must follow through with your enemy. If you leave your throat exposed, it will be slit."

Brigit at once, picked up a stick and began to emulate Gunnar's movements. He whirled around often to smack Og on various parts of his body.

"I am just not fast enough," cried Og. He bent over and placed a hand on his knee to catch his breath. He looked down-hearted.

"You are not yet, but you will be," Gunnar encouraged him. "Try with this girl. She has had some training," Gunnar held Brigit, from behind, by her shoulders and whispered in her ear, "A man has told me of his love-sickness for you. Watch your window for a visitor one night soon." Then he said out loud, "Let us see how you are matched." He winked at her and pushed Brigit toward Og.

"We will see," Og bent his knees and took a wide stance. He and Brigit were a good match for practice. She was faster, but he had more strength and therefore more power behind his swings. They parried until Og asked to stop for a rest. He wearily went to sit near the water pail and drank his fill, then splashed his face and neck with water.

Gunnar went to sit next to Nora and kissed her neck. She cooed and patted him happily with a brilliant smile. He slid down on the dark brown earth and put his head in her lap. Nora gladly laid down her nalbinding in favor of stroking his hair while they watched the young women and their sword practice.

Brigit turned to Freyja and they began to work together, using their sticks as swords. Freyja was picking up the movement of sword work quickly. They were also becoming quick at anticipating each other's movements and blocked one stick with the other. Soon the sticks were broken into pieces. Brigit threw hers down in disgust.

"We need to get something better to use than these sticks," said Brigit.

"I will ask in the village about some wooden swords that are used for training," said Gunnar. "I have been sworn to secrecy about training Og, but I could ask for some for young shield-maidens," he laughed.

"Do not do that," responded Freyja anxiously. "I do not want people having something to say or making fun of us. I will find something." She was thinking of the old brothers and their forge.

Chapter Eighteen

At the end of a long day, Gunnar gave Og a ride to the village on his horse. Nora was none too happy to lose time with Gunnar, but Arndis was relieved to have the household back to normal and Brigit was happy to return to a bed.

Around the evening fire Nora spoke of the training. "These young women have the makings of warriors!" she said with gusto between mouthfuls of boiled potatoes.

"What are you talking about?" Arndis laughed. "Freyja has had no teacher and has no weapons, but her knife."

"Brigit has shown me the sling and now she teaches me the sword. Today Gunnar and Og helped us, as well," replied Freyja. Her jaw set with indignation that her mother might doubt her potential. "Now we hope to find something better to work with than sticks," said Freyja.

"I wish you luck with learning this, honestly. There is no doubt that we might need such skills on a farm of only women. Your grandfather would be proud and would have trained you himself," Arndis paused. "I will ask for his advice as I dream tonight." She reached for the warrior's mushroom on her shelf and began to make a tea to help her dream. She had made it for her father, but only made a small dose for herself. After drinking it she took Freyja to her room and spoke quietly. "I will need the bed to myself for dreaming. Take what skins you need to make your bed."

Freyja did not mind being put out. She felt that it would be a nice night to sleep under the stars so made a small fire and a pleasant bed for herself near the barn. She was happy to be away from the house and the people. Happy to be alone in the quiet. She snuggled down in her furs and quickly dozed off as the fire died down.

In the darkness she heard the animals in the barn stirring and moments later, footfalls. She held her breath as a figure passed on the way to the house. Near her mother's window, where Brigit and Nora now slept, it stopped. A man's voice whispered, "I wait for you in the barn." Freyja knew the voice. It was Sven.

Halfway back to the barn, Freyja stepped in front of him. "You will meet no one tonight." She put her hand on her knife.

"You would use your knife on me?" Sven asked horrified.

"I just might," she answered fiercely.

"Do you hate me so?" he sounded incredulous.

"Sven." She tilted her head to the heavens then shook it in disbelief as she brought it down to look into his eyes. "Once you were my life, my fortune, and my only future. I loved you fiercely, above all others. Then my sister...I mean this woman, came and all changed. You changed. Now you flaunt this infatuation in front of me. You who listened to Captain Gunnar say, 'You will guard the Irish chief's daughter. No harm will befall her, no man will lay hands upon her.' Now you will lay hands on her? Not tonight. I will guard Brigit as I would myself. You will have to amuse yourself, alone this night. Leave this farm now. My kin is under my protection." She stepped aside, out of his path. He opened his mouth, as if to speak, then closed it. His face fell, but he walked on.

A few moments later Freyja watched Brigit walk stealthily to the barn. She carried a skin. She did not leave. Freyja hoped that Brigit waited long for Sven and then fell asleep, alone.

Freyja slept fitfully. She dreamt of her grandparents dancing as her grandmother murmured the words *"inn matki munr"* over and over. They looked so happy together. Then she dreamt of her mother and her father, as she envisioned him, together laughing as they walked the farm. She then dreamt of herself as the goddess and Sven as a fallen warrior. It was the recurring dream she had many times, only the dream was not passionate or inspiring as it had been at first. Again, Sven left her bed without sharing himself. She woke alone and feeling alone. She felt that she might never know the mighty passion.

She woke and checked to see that her fire was out, gathering up her skins. When she walked in to check the cooking pot over the fire, Nora came out of her room. "Brigit must be up early to tend the animals."

"I believe she is in the barn," Freyja smiled a half-hearted smile.

"I had such dreams last night," Nora continued. "Gunnar stood at my window saying, 'I wait for you in the barn'. Such a silly man, as he knows this bed is very comfortable," she laughed.

Freyja responded, "It must be the goddess *Nott*. I had strange dreams, as well"

Arndis came to the fire. She looked tired though her eyes were shining. "And what of your dreaming, mother?" Freyja asked.

"I saw both my parents and they were dancing. Mother was speaking of the mighty passion as she often would. They made me laugh. It felt like the farm was good and all was well," Arndis sighed happily.

"Did you speak to Grandfather about my training?" Freja interjected.

"He brought it up and said that he knew you would be a proud shield-maiden and it was about time that you learned," Arndis replied.

Freyja smiled, but still asked, "And?"

Arndis said, "He said that you should have his weapons and train hard!"

"Weapons, here? We have Grandfather's weapons?" Freyja had never thought about this before.

Arndis took Freyja into her bedroom. "You know this was my parents' bed before it was mine, yes?" Freyja nodded. "Help me move it," Arndis commanded.

She and Freyja pushed the bed aside to reveal a trap door. Arndis pulled it up to lean it against the bed. She kneeled on the floor and reached down to pull up a leather-bound bundle. Arndis nodded and Freyja opened it with trembling fingers. Inside there was a dagger and a sword. Both had the same hilt with an oval piece on top. They had a carved bluish design that she recognized, but could not place.

"These will need to be sharpened," said Arndis solemnly as she ran her finger gingerly down the blades.

Brigit and Nora had entered the room and stood quietly as they watched. Once more Arndis reached down to bring up a shield. The wood seemed good, but well scarred. The leather handle would need to be replaced as well as the metal boss in the center and the metal edging. Freyja could hardly believe her eyes as her mother, yet again, reached in. She brought forth an axe with leather bindings.

Brigit knelt in awe and Freyja touched each item reverently. These had belonged to the last warrior in their family and now he had given them to her. She was overwhelmed with gratitude and responsibility.

"I will care for these and learn to use these well," she spoke barely above a whisper. "I must go and give thanks to the gods and to my grandfather," Freyja said feeling moved to go to her altar. They put the items back in their hiding place and pushed the bed back in place.

Chapter Nineteen

Freyja walked slowly to her meadow and to her grey stone altar. She was not sure how to thank her grandfather and the gods so she started by sitting in front of her altar. She closed her eyes and was filled with a sense of purpose. No longer was she for Sven. She was for her people; her family, her village. As a shield-maiden she could protect what she valued and loved. She felt sure her grandfather would approve.

Suddenly she remembered her grandfather's blue tattoo of Freyja's cats. He would laugh and tell her, "Here are your kittens. They will pull you out of any trouble." She had been gifted these weapons, with the same markings, by her grandfather and they would pull her out of any trouble as the goddess' grey-blue cats pulled her chariot.

She knelt before her altar and lifted her face, with closed eyes. "I pledge the gift of my grandfather's weapons to the protection of my people. I will learn to use them swiftly and with purpose. I am forever grateful for this gift." She stayed still for a long time.

When she arose, she went to her mother in the garden. Freyja's face was serious so Arndis stood and waited for her to speak.

"I have pledged my protection to our people. I will use Grandfather's blue kittens to pull us out of any trouble," Freyja said with the glint of her grandfather's memory in her eyes.

Arndis' eyes filled with tears, "Oh yes, he would say that. You have heard his wishes." She hugged Freyja fiercely. "Now you must train in order to use these gifts well. In time we must share the news. We should seek the counsel of the Old One."

Freyja looked for her sister. She was in the barn, finished with the milking of the goats and cow. "Here you are in time to take a bucket," Brigit thrust a bucket in Freyja's hand while she shooed the animals outside.

The little goat herd had grown in size. The two nannies had three kids each, weaned and grown well. The billy goat was constantly trying to stay away from all who butted him fiercely. They were all happy to be outside and ate every plant available to them, except the garden Freyja had wisely protected with a low fence.

Freyja and Brigit took the buckets inside and started to make goat cheese. Brigit tried not to pry then fairly burst asking, "What did you learn at your altar? Do you have your grandfather's blessing? What of our training? Are you to be a shield-maiden?"

Freyja laughed heartily and placed her hand on Brigit's shoulder. "I have pledged my protection to my people. I must train and learn if I am to be a shield-maiden."

Gunnar came through the door, just at that moment. "What is this talk of shield-maidens? That is why I am here. Well, that and Nora," he slapped his thigh. "Give me food and then we train. I have wooden swords outside." They gave him bread and fresh milk and let him rest briefly before pulling him off the bench.

They passed by the garden fence, wooden swords in hand. Arndis waved in greeting while Nora leaned over for an embrace, but Gunnar quickly pulled away. "I have no time now, as you see. These fierce shield-maidens will have me work."

Arndis asked, "What of Og? Does he come here today?"

Gunnar replied, "He works with young Klause and Karle for some time. They are equally matched in skill and all know now of Og's training."

"Then be off to your training. If it goes late, then you must stay the night on the farm, yes?" Nora's voice went up.

"Yes!" Gunnar bellowed with delight. "Do not worry Brigit. We will bed in the barn tonight and you may keep your bed," he said with a wink.

Gunnar started by making sure the girls were holding their swords correctly. Then he worked on their stance for face-to-face close combat. He talked about vulnerable parts of the body and how to protect them. He explained how the female body often has a lower center of gravity and their height and less upper body strength might put them at a disadvantage against a man. To counter this, he had them work on side-to-side movements and getting their opponent off balance. An ultimate goal would be the strengthening of their upper bodies.

Brigit tired of his teaching, "So much talk. When do we fight?"

"You are training now, which means learning. I often teach by talking, but I can show you." Gunnar took Freyja's wooden sword and approached Brigit. She expertly blocked his thrust and quickly dodged to the side to miss a blow. She then became overconfident and was knocked off her feet ending with Gunnar holding his sword to her throat.

She lay panting on the ground, red faced, and not just a little chagrined, "All right, lesson learned," Brigit said. "Freyja, I say we are to the creek." She pulled Freyja's arm to help herself up and they ran together laughing while Gunnar shook his head.

"Tomorrow, we train twice as hard," he yelled after them.

Once at the creek the girls waded in to cool off. It was getting too cold to jump in all the way and it cooled them quickly. Freyja splashed her face and sat down on the bank, "You did well with Gunnar. I will learn this and we will train more outside before the snows. My mother says I will soon need to tell the village of my pledge."

"You worry that they will not accept this?" asked Brigit as she sat on the creek bank.

"Many people doubt me now that the prophecy has changed. They do not know what to make of me and neither do I," Freyja admitted with some sadness in her voice.

"But now you do. You have made a pledge," smiled Brigit reassuringly.

"And you. What of your plans?" asked Freyja.

"Me? I have made no pledge. I am to stay alive until I am ransomed and then return to the house of my father," Brigit looked at Freyja to see if she had wounded her. "I mean our father." They each touched their necklaces at the same time. Both smiled. "Perhaps you will come with me or come later. You should see it," sighed Brigit.

Freyja stood and grabbed Brigit's arm to pull her up beside her, "Perhaps."

The sun started it's descent as they walked home. Each seemed lost in her own thoughts and the silence was comfortable. When they got to the fire Arndis, Gunnar, and Nora were at the table. They visited about the day's training and how the girls were beginning to use the wooden swords. No one mentioned Freyja's pledge or her grandfather's weapons to Gunnar. It was Freyja's place to speak of these.

After they had eaten Arndis excused herself. "I am tired, so I am to bed."

"I am not tired, but I am to bed. Bring skins to keeps us warm, Nora," smiled Gunnar. She had already gotten them and stood at the doorway. They left quickly for the barn laughing and talking as they went.

"I was wondering if it was cold in the barn," said Freyja. "I saw you walk by my sleeping place the night of my mother's dreaming. You slept in the barn?"

"Yes," answered Brigit not looking at her.

"I thought I heard a man's invitation for you to join him there," said Freyja.

"I thought so too, but he was not there and he did not come," said Brigit tearing up. "I think he was just teasing me or maybe it was a dream as Nora said. I know you do not like it for me to see Sven, but I feel a pull between us." She broke down in tears.

Freyja sighed and put her finger under Brigit's chin. She lifted her face and searched her eyes. "*Eigi leyna augu ef ann kona manni.*' Eyes cannot hide a woman's love for a man," she quoted the saga. Freyja took her hand away, "No, I do not like it that you see Sven. You may feel for him, but we cannot know how he feels and he has pledged to protect you. Gunnar has said, no harm will befall you, no man will lay hands upon you." Brigit looked torn. Pleased of protection and limited by it as well.

"We will sleep with these thoughts. Good night, Brigit, daughter of Brion." She held up her half coin and Brigit did the same.

Chapter Twenty

In a few days the morning was frosty and Arndis, Freyja, and Brigit sat for a long time by the fire. "Mother, I want to take Grandfather's weapons to be mended and sharpened. The ax handle needs new leather and the shield needs to be mended," Freyja broached the idea.

"Yes, I myself saw the need of this," Arndis replied. "Whom do you trust?"

"The old brothers, Hallr and Kofri, have spoken to me about their knowledge of the forge and weapons. I would like to ask them," Freyja stated.

"And where do you find them?" Arndis questioned.

"I have only seen them at the Mead House. I will start there," replied Freyja.

"After we do the chores and care for the farm, you will take the horse to the village to do so. I want you also to seek out the Old One and ask her to consult the gods about your pledge." Freyja nodded. She adjusted the cheese board and made sure the whey was draining into the crock they would use for fermenting roots. "You will take a gift of cheese to the Old One."

Brigit wanted to go with her, but Freyja explained to her, "I must tell of my pledge myself and I may need to spend the night in the village." Brigit set her jaw angrily and nodded. She felt that Freyja wanted to insure she had no contact with Sven and while that might have truth to it, it was far from Freyja's busy mind.

Brigit and Freyja went to the barn to find Nora and Gunnar wrapped in a passionate embrace. "Oh, Odin! We will be back soon to tend to the animals," spat Brigit, turning around while covering her eyes with her hands.

"So, you are calling on our gods now?" asked Freyja.

"Well, as sisters we can share much," laughed Brigit as they looked for eggs outside of the barn.

"I find only two so will take these in my pouch," Freyja noted. "Besides, we will be filling our buckets with milk." Freyja started for the barn just as Gunnar and Nora burst out of the door. The cow mooed its good bye.

"We are out of your way girls. Come get me when you are ready to train," Gunnar chased after Nora who was giggling on her way to the house. They had left one skin, warm on the hay. Freyja ran her hand over it and felt the warmth from their body heat. The memory of her night in the barn with Sven flooded her. Her chest tightened as she breathed in the feelings of that night, long ago. She quickly looked at Brigit to see if she had seen; Fortunately, she had gone straight to the cow and was filling the bucket.

When their buckets were full, they let the animals out to forage for food. The full buckets went inside to provide milk for breakfast, butter, and maybe some for cheese. Nora and Gunnar were still smiling stupidly at each other and Arndis was pretending to ignore them. "We will work on some tactics today, so eat and we will train," commanded Gunnar.

"I will need Nora's help with the milk," said Arndis.

"That is good with me," smiled Nora. "I am tired and I will be happy to make butter."

Gunnar picked up the wooden swords and danced out the door while singing. Freyja raised her eyebrows at Brigit and tried not to laugh. Brigit was unable to hold her laughter and giggled as she followed Gunnar down the steps. He took one of the swords and wacked her on the bottom. In doing so he dropped the other and she picked it up. They began their battle around the well and Freyja watched, entertained.

"Now watch," Gunnar yelled. He reached down and grabbed a handful of frosty earth and threw it in Brigit's face, on the right side of the well. When she was reacting, he came around the left side and her back. He brought his sword to her throat. "Drop your sword," Gunnar said. "Pick it up, Freyja," he yelled. She did and the lesson continued.

They fought to the garden fence where he took a log from the fence and threw it at Freyja. She dodged it and came at him again with her sword. Gunnar went behind the corner of the house. Freyja nodded to Brigit and she went around from the other side. Freyja came at Gunnar, throwing rocks to distract his attention, but he did not take the bait. In the meantime, Brigit had come up behind him. She ran at him and threw her weight against him so that he was pushed out in front of Freyja. Brigit grabbed him around the waist and he dragged her as he confronted Freya. Freyja could not help laughing and knelt on the ground as she held herself up with the wooden sword. "Do not laugh, little one. This can happen in battle, though it may not be your sister," Gunnar lay down on the ground dragging Brigit with him.

He seemed to rest and Brigit relaxed her hold on him. He laughed, "Never trust your adversary!" Gunnar rolled away from Brigit and stood behind Freyja who was still kneeling, with his sword poised above her shoulders. Freyja threw her sword to Brigit and there appeared to be a stand-off. "You should yield, or lose your sister!" Gunnar yelled at Brigit. Brigit put her sword down and kicked it to Gunnar. He kicked it up with his toes to catch it in his free hand and now had a sword pointed at each girl. "I am victorious," Gunnar smiled comically.

Nora and Arndis had been attracted to the battle sound and were watching out the window. "I am not sure you are ready for battle," Arndis called out, shaking her head, but smiling.

Nora yelled, "You are all filthy, covered with mud. You will not enter the house or my bed as such. Strip at the door and I will make you a bath."

"Who shall go first?" asked Gunnar.

"Smallest first," offered Freyja and pushed Brigit toward the door. Freyja drew a bucket of water from the well and passed it through the doorway to Nora. It quickly came back empty and she filled it again and again as it was called for.

Brigit sat on the steps laughing, "Captain Gunnar, today I have learned to close my eyes when dirt is thrown and that you are hard to hold on to."

"But you hung on well. Just look for someone with a waist the size of mine, or smaller," he laughed.

"Freyja, come help Brigit," Nora called and Freyja held Brigit's clothes as she left them on the steps and went to a warm bath.

Freyja looked seriously at Gunnar and said, "When I am clean, I go to the village." Gunnar nodded. "I ask for the blessing of the gods to become a shield-maiden. I will ask the Old One to seek guidance," Freyja finished.

Gunnar nodded again, "Are you prepared for this?"

"Yes," Freyja answered. "My grandfather has given me his weapons in a dream to my mother. I will take them for repair and sharpening."

"Do you want me to come with you?" asked Gunnar.

"No. I must do this alone," Freyja responded

"Good," nodded Gunnar, "I will stay with Nora."

"Freyja, more water. And you may have your turn," yelled Nora from inside.

Freyja brought a bucket inside with her, forgetting her muddy clothing.

"No, no. No clothes inside. Strip and throw them on the steps." Freyja did so, forgetting that Gunnar was there. He was appreciative, but quiet.

Freyja bathed and went to sit on her bed. The warm water had calmed her and she felt ready to go the village, even though she was not sure of the progression of the visit. Brigit soon came to join her, clean as well, "I wish you good fortune on your visit to the village. You know that I will help you any way I can. Our future is bound together, I know it," Brigit said.

Freyja patted her hand asking, "Then I may borrow your cloak? My shawl has come apart."

"Of course, sister," Brigit said with a small smile.

Freyja soon readied the horse and tested the wrappings on the the weapons. Weapons and the shield were tied to the horse's blanket. The women all bade her good faring and Gunnar waved from the bath.

Freyja wrapped Brigit's cloak around her shoulders and put the hood over her head to protect against the chill air. She carried her grandfather's weapons along with her hopes. She planned to go to the Mead House and look for the elder brothers, Hallr and Kofri. They could tell her what should be done to bring the metal back to life. They may also know about the leather wrap on the axe and the work needed on the shield.

When she got to the Mead House she slid down from the horse and busied herself with untying the bundle. She felt hands on her shoulders and turned around.

"Oh, I am sorry. The cloak. I thought you were Brigit," Sven stammered. He had made an error assuming the woman was the owner of the cloak.

"I am not," stated Freyja without a smile. She turned back to the horse and continued to untie her bundle. She moved around Sven to enter and find the brothers.

They were seated, as always, at the table of old men. The dark eyed beauty she had seen visiting with the old men before was again sitting with them and speaking to one of them in the strange language. The woman started to get up, but Freyja motioned her to stay. Freyja placed her bundle on the table in front of the brothers. "Can you make these new?" she asked them and slowly opened the skin.

The brothers both sucked in a breath and smiled broadly when they saw the weapons. "I know these. We worked on these for your grandfather," said Hallr.

"Yes," Kofri mused, "I carved Freyja's cats on the hilt of the dagger and sword." He picked up the dagger and examined it. He held it against his large crooked nose to sight down its length. "We can clean and sharpen these. The axe will need new leather bindings as well. We will ask for help with the wood of the shield." Both old men smiled.

"Who will use these?" asked Kofri.

Freyja took a deep breath and answered, "I will." The old men looked at each other knowingly and nodded.

The slave girl reached out her hand and touched the sword with reverence. She looked wistful and stood up to leave. She moved her dark hair over her shoulder slowly and proudly. She nodded to them all and went back to her work. "She looks sad," noted Freyja.

"She longs for her own sword once again," Kofri volunteered.

"But slaves cannot own weapons," gasped Freyja.

Hallr pointed with his chin at the wall, "Hers is there." On the wall hung a curved sword. Freyja had only looked on it as a decoration before and had never thought to ask about it. "How is it, and how is she, here?" Freyja asked.

Hallr continued. "Halig, the owner of the Mead House, brought her back as a slave after one of his trips down the Dnieper River. She fought against him and his men who were trading in the Black Sea area. She was a warrior and a woman. She claims she is descended from Babak and Banu, though I do not know if this is so. They were a couple with a great love and reputation. They battled on horseback against conquerors who brought with them a new religion. She fought well until her capture. Halig chose not to kill her so he took her for a slave. He made a pledge to her that after eight years or his death, whichever comes first, she will have her freedom."

"And her sword," added Kofri. "Her name is Fereshte. It means 'messenger of the gods' in Persian. She is always kind to us. She likes to speak with those who know her language from their travels."

Freyja took in the story. "So, there are shield-maidens in other places."

"Yes, and we will help you become such. First your weapons will be made ready." Hallr and Kofri wrapped the bundle up again with care. Kofri carried the axe and shield. They walked slowly to the door and nodded good bye to Freyja. The open door showed the setting sun fire the sky with brilliant orange colors. Freyja took it as a good omen.

She also felt good about her elder friends working on the weapons that they knew. It seemed that her grandfather's blessing was laid upon her plan. Now to find the Old One for more blessings.

Freyja turned around on the bench to look over the Mead House. It was not a busy night as more people would be near their home fires in the cool evenings after harvest. She saw Sven sitting with some of his friends. He looked back at her and she felt a bitterness overtake her. She reminded herself that her fortunes were changing. No longer was she part of Sven's life. After a few breaths she calmed herself and stood.

She walked toward Sven and took some more breaths to steady herself. "Have you seen the Old One? I need her counsel."

Sven was visibly surprised by her approach. He stood, "I saw her today with her family in the village."

"Can you speak to her to say that I must have her read the runes?" asked Freyja, "and give her this cheese."

"I will and I will bring her to your farm when she is ready to meet with you," Sven offered. Freyja thought briefly that, of course, he would want to come to the farm, but she said nothing.

"Thank you," she said softly.

Outside she breathed in the sharp cool air. She had started her transformation to shield-maiden. A few small steps had been taken and with the gods help, she would be successful. She mounted her horse feeling good about this night. Her stomach rumbled and she was ready to go home. She would have to trust that Sven would do as he promised. The darkness moved in, close like a comfortable blanket, and the horse took her home.

Chapter Twenty-One

When she got to the farm, she put the horse in the barn to find that Gunnar's horse was still there. By the fire she found bread and nearby was fresh butter and some radishes from the garden. She put butter on the bread and sliced radishes on top for her late nattmal. She chewed thoughtfully and wondered at their relative prosperity.

The infamous cow had become a valued part of the farm and was proof. She had erroneously thought it had been offered by Og for her virginity last spring. In the past her mother, Arndis, had traded sexual favors with Og regularly. Og had continually said that he would trade a cow if he could be Freyja's first lover. Freyja had previously been protected from joining her mother's profession because of her part in the prophecy, but last spring the village people had begun to challenge the prophecy. When Freyja found the cow in their barn, she assumed that her mother had traded her to Og for a night. Freyja angrily replied that she would not accept the cow as she and Sven had been together, the prophecy begun.

The cow had, in fact, been a gift from Arndis' lover Tahir. Since the cow had arrived pregnant, she had produced not only a she calf, but plenty of milk for them. That milk made butter and sometimes cheese. Both meant left over whey was available to ferment their garden vegetables. Such vegetables typically carried their people through the winter and were often sent with the village men on their vikings in the spring.

She sighed contentedly. The house was full now, but that was not a bad thing. Freyja looked down to notice a pile of skins near the fire and made a sour face. She tiptoed to find Brigit in the bed with her mother and her suspicions were confirmed. Nora now shared her own bed often with Gunnar. The fire side bed had been left for Freyja.

They may have thought she would stay in the village. No matter. They had left plentiful skins and she snuggled down close to the low light of the fire. Her eyes closed and she began to dream. A woman with dark beautiful eyes was a vision before her. Then the recurring dream began. This time Sven the Norse warrior was accompanied by a dark woman from the eastern lands. She wore a sword at her waist that curved and her clothing was very colorful. Her dark hair flowed around her and she moved smoothly, entering the hall, *Sessrumnir*. They both sat at the long table, abundantly laden with all manner of foods and began to eat and drink with Freyja, *Valkyries*, and other fallen warriors.

Freyja, as the goddess, retired to her bed as she watched all the warriors satisfy their appetites. She pushed herself back against the wall and opened herself to call a warrior to her. Sven got up and walked toward her. At the foot of the bed, he saw the trunk laden with silver and gold. He stopped, closed the lid, picked it up and walked out of the hall. Freyja's mouth fell open, but for some reason she did not feel surprise.

The other warriors began to fall asleep drunken, at the table, their stomachs full. All but the woman warrior. She walked slowly and purposefully to the foot of Freyja's bed. Her eyes met Freyja's and she laid her sword on the floor. She put one knee on the bed and began to crawl toward Freyja with her chin held high and a hungry fire burning in her sable eyes.

Waking sharply from the dream, Freyja wondered what it could mean. She knew Sven was mostly interested in what he could now gain from the prophecy, which was in the words "trade and prosper." Taking the chest would be the symbol. But what of the words, "When Freyja and Sven couple"? Of course, he now wanted Brigit. Freyja lay with these feelings: betrayal, bitterness, loss.

And what of this woman? Her tired brain could not think on this and she closed her eyes. As she fell back asleep, she saw a face, with olive complexion and dark brown eyes, swim before her. She felt comforted by this face and seemed to know it. The feelings led her to a restful sleep.

Chapter Twenty-Two

"Freyja, wake. Og is here for training and Gunnar says we may join them," Brigit shook Freyja by the shoulder.

"No need to hurry. We should eat well before we work so hard. I also have just walked this long way," Og settled himself on a bench, his eyes searching for food.

Gunnar sat next to him chiding, "Not every day will bring food on your journey, Og."

"I will take nourishment when I can, then," replied Og.

Nora came out, "Ach, we will see what we have for this dagmal. Your stomach is always busy even if you are not." She shook her head, "Here is bread and butter." She tore the bread into pieces. Arndis came through the door with a skirt full of eggs and the problem of the meal was solved when they boiled the eggs. They tossed their eggs from hand to hand as they cooled which made Brigit laugh gleefully. Then Gunnar continued the show of peeling his eggs with a great flourish. After all had eaten well, Gunnar stood and hurried them along.

"We train now in the cool of the autumn weather. It will make for more energy! Today the ground is dry and your footing will be sure. You are all improving so you will all try with your wooden swords." He held the door urging Og along, "Now, my friend. You will pick up your sword instead of the bread." Og got up slowly and stretched. He was obviously delaying his move away from the fire. He winked at Arndis and Nora then sauntered to the door. Gunnar almost pushed him out, "The girls are faster than you. Remember you must be ready for the ship that leaves this spring."

"I know, I know. I will have a ship full of comrades to defend me," smiled Og, unconcerned.

Gunnar scowled, "They are not your caretakers, Og. They will depend on you as well."

Og looked down at his round belly and thought a moment. "I have been reminded of my past glory and I think I will do well. I will have all of winter to train."

Gunnar looked thoughtful. It was true that Og had begun to move more smoothly and quickly. He held his weapons well and had regained the upper body strength to wield them. These last weeks had been good for Og and the girls as well. He hoped that Og would be ready to fiercely defend himself and others. When the ice begins to break the ship would need to be leaving with Og aboard, ready, or not.

"Today, Og, you will fight with Brigit." They were each given their wooden swords and Gunnar yelled at them, "Watch your feet, guard your sides." They focused on each other and were not giving the other an inch leeway. Gunnar approached Freyja in a whisper. "Sneak around behind Og to attack him from the rear."

She came up behind Og but he had developed a twisting pattern so did not keep his back to her. He reacted to her and took on both girls. They were all blocking each other's thrusts and not landing any decisive blows. After a time of this, Gunnar called a halt. He had them pick up the practice spears they had made and begin to throw at their targets on the edge of the forest. They were all increasing their distance, accuracy, and force. Sweat appeared on each brow, but Gunnar continued urging them on. He had them trade targets and then had them run past while throwing. In short order they were tiring, but still he kept them moving until they heard a loud shout, "Hold!"

They all stopped in their tracks and shielded their eyes to look past their targets into the dim forest. Three beautiful men emerged from the foliage. One dark, one fair, and one ruddy. Freyja ran up to the dark and tallest of them in greeting. "Tahir," she shouted happily and patted his shoulder with her free arm.

Og also cheered up, dropping his spear. He stepped forward to yell the name. "Tahir. You have saved me from these *Valkyries.* Welcome." The two men embraced. Brigit put down her spear also as training appeared to be over.

"What goes on here?" asked Tahir of Og.

"I am in training for a spring ransom voyage and these young women will be shield-maidens," answered Og.

Tahir raised his eyebrows, "You are no longer a young man Og."

"The Old One cast the runes and I was chosen. It is my destiny so I must ready," Og seemed pleased with himself as he straightened his tunic.

"We came up your path thinking it might lead to the village. Your ship and new ice kept us from getting to the path I know to be to the village," continued Tahir. "Our ship is on your beach with our goods being guarded by the rest of our crew. We hope to enjoy some company and trade a bit in your village before heading to our homes for a winter of rest." Freyja looked at his two companions and noticed that they too had colorful beads in the locks of their hair (this had been Tahir's distinguishing mark, in his black hair, when he came to the village last spring). She met the eyes of the fair blond giant and they both smiled and nodded. He had an open face and she liked him immediately. She turned to look at the other, a man with red flowing beard and freckled complexion. His blue eyes were piercing and he held her gaze for a bit too long. There was an undeniable attraction between them. She felt a stirring in the pit of her stomach and caught her breath.

Turning quickly back to Tahir she offered, "My mother will be happy to see you, Tahir," and she dropped her spear to put her arm around Tahir's waist. "Let us to the house."

Og began reminding Gunnar and telling these two new men of his long friendship with Tahir and how Tahir, the Moor, had come to their village last spring after they had not seen each other for many years. He told how he had gotten over his jealousy of Tahir when Arndis had made it plain that she would no longer see Og even if he brought a cow in payment. "It seems Tahir has stolen her heart and she will have no other. He indeed bought his own cow to send to her farm," Og said with a straight face.

All the men walked toward the house with Freyja leading. Brigit looked around and realized she was left to gather the spears and wooden swords. She made disgusted faces as she carried the large bundle toward the house. She felt she could use a break and when she got to the well, she unceremoniously dumped the wooden weapons and stopped for a long drink of water.

Laughter spilled out of the house and Brigit sat on the steps to listen to the talk. She learned that Tahir and his friends would stay on the farm tonight and had dried fruits and wine from the south to share for tonight's *nattmal*. They had all met in the great center of Hedeby where goods and slaves from all over the world were traded. Tahir had met their captain and joined their crew when he heard they would be sailing to this village. "I asked if I might pay for my ship space and trade my wine and dried fruits. I told him I was wanting to return after my visit here last year," Tahir said with a wide grin and wink directed at Arndis. "And I am happy to be back with the 'other half of my orange'," Tahir said as he embraced Arndis playfully. He continued to whisper the lovers' phrase from his homeland close to her ear.

"The captain told me he had heard rumors of a captive that was sure to bring the village riches upon ransom and he hoped that the villagers would have wealth to trade for his goods," continued Tahir from within the circle of Arndis' arms. The fair and red haired men both exchanged eager glances.

Og told them that the wealth was yet to be obtained and that he, in fact, would be going to get it. "The people may be willing to part with trade items knowing that I will return with greater wealth for all," Og boasted. "We will leave in the spring when the weather and the ice breaks," he nodded with assurance.

Brigit stepped into the room and Og bellowed, "Here is our captive now."

"She walks freely?" Tahir was surprised.

"She is not only a captive, she is my sister," Freyja said solemnly and went to stand beside Brigit. "I will tell you the story of how we learned of this later," Freyja promised.

Tahir just shook his head and widened his eyes. "I see something of you in her. She seems to train hard to be a good warrior as well as you do," added Tahir with approval.

"We are learning with Og as he prepares to go and negotiate the ransom. Gunnar is giving us his knowledge and making us work very hard," Freyja shared.

"Well enough of work today, Og. It is time for you to return to the village. I will give you a ride," volunteered Gunnar, stretching as he stood. Gunnar and Og promised to spread the word of the traders.

They had brought wine, grain, and dried fruits from the south to trade. They were hoping to get good furs like fox and would take amber and even dried fish in trade. They would like nuts and fruit from the local harvest as well. They would return to their village for the winter and then take the trip south to the Black Sea when the Dnieper River thawed.

Gunnar embraced Nora and whispered in her ear, "I hope you will not be too cold without me in your bed." He looked pointedly at the visitors.

"Don't worry, I promise to be cold until you return," Nora patted him on the butt. She took his hand to walk him outside and watched while he readied his horse.

"What of the red wine from the south? I would like to taste it," Og spoke loudly enough for Gunnar to hear. He did not want to leave without trying the wine, but Gunnar came back inside to drag him out.

"We have news to share and Helga will want you home," Gunnar took Og by the elbow and walked behind him down the steps.

"There is more on the ship, Og," Tahir yelled as Og departed. Tahir looked to Arndis and laughed, "Now indeed there will be enough for the rest of us."

Chapter Twenty-Three

Tahir insisted on checking Freyja's snares with her as they had last spring when they first met. They walked out and Brigit followed. Freyja told Tahir the story of how she and Brigit had discovered that they were sisters through the coins they wore around their necks. Perhaps leaving out some of her more childish behavior.

"The half coin that I made fun of?" Tahir asked.

"Yes, just so," answered Freyja. She took hers out of her blouse and Brigit did the same.

"This is surely the doing of the gods," Tahir nodded.

Freyja also shared about her path to becoming a shield-maiden. She felt close enough to him to even speak of her pledge to protect her people. He nodded his approval as she spoke. "I believe the gods favor you," he said.

Brigit quietly released rabbits from three of the snares and dispatched them while Tahir and Freyja talked. More of the snares were empty, so Freyja reset them. The last of the snares, the farthest from the farm, showed signs again that the catch had been taken; blood and fur remained. Freyja shook her head and laughed, launching into the tale of how

Brigit had saved her from a wolf some weeks ago. Tahir looked impressed. "The she wolf ran yelping into the forest after Brigit pelted it," remembered Freyja. "Her jumping up and down may have also frightened it," she laughed.

"How do you, privileged woman, come to have such knowledge of slings and snares?" he asked Brigit with interest.

"My father came home from this village to have a family on the Far Isle. I was pushed to the kitchen and loom, but always wanted to follow my brother. My father could not say no to me, so I learned with my brother," replied Brigit rather proudly.

"Well tomorrow we will test these skills of yours. And of you Freyja? To become a shield-maiden you must have skills and knowledge, also. Let me help you. But first to the fire to cook these fine rabbits."

The three made their way back to the farm to find Tahir's friends outside sharpening their knives. Freyja watched with interest as they showed the edges were sharp enough to shave the hair on their forearms. There was a pattern on the metal that made her think of the sand on the beach at first light. Tahir explained, "We found these knives in the area of the Black Sea. They are not iron nor bronze and hold an edge like no other. Have you real weapons, not only your wooden swords and spears?" Freyja told him more of her guidance from the gods to pledge to protect her people as a shield-maiden and then told of the blessing of her grandfather's weapons.

Tahir asked, "Can you show me these?"

"They are in the village being mended and sharpened. I will get them soon. I wait for the blessing and guidance of the Old One, as well. Sven had promised to bring her to me when last I was in the village." She looked quickly at Brigit whose head had snapped up when she heard the name, Sven.

"So, I will see these soon," determined Tahir.

Brigit had been skinning and cleaning the rabbits while she listened, throwing the entrails to the chickens. Now she took meat in to the pot over the fire. Freyja also went inside to ask her mother what had come from the garden this day and to start a stew. Brigit lowered her eyes to speak to Freyja, "You spoke with Sven?"

"Yes, I did not see the Old One at the Mead House so asked him to give her my message. I must have her cast the runes to find the fate of my quest as a shield-maiden," replied Freyja.

"Was he well?" continued Brigit.

"He looked fine, drinking and laughing with his friends," answered Freyja curtly. Sven was not a subject that she wanted to discuss with Brigit so she turned to Arndis. "I will show the men where they can sleep tonight in the barn. And Tahir? Is he still welcome in your bed?"

Arndis smiled broadly, "Of course, I welcome him."

"Then I will sleep elsewhere," Freyja responded.

Freyja went to show the men where to put their bags and gave them a few furs. As they walked to the barn, Freyja shared details about the farm. The two men looked over the property carefully and listened. They nodded approvingly.

Freyja was talking a bit too quickly and realized she was feeling flustered by the close attention that Red Eric was paying to her. He listened as his eyes rarely left hers. Her eyes locked on his and she stumbled. Red Eric reached a strong arm out to steady her quickly and she fell into his strong embrace. She laughed nervously and stood up slowly savoring the warmth of his arms. It had been a long time since she had been embraced by a man.

She turned to hide her blush and left the men to set up their sleeping area. She was smiling girlishly when she neared the fire to check on the stew.

"What is this?" Brigit asked of Freyja.

"Oh, we were laughing," said Freyja.

"Tell me. What is funny?" asked Brigit.

"I tripped while walking to the barn. It was, just funny," replied Freyja. Brigit pursed her lips and looked at Freyja as if she were crazy.

When the stew was ready, Nora went to tell Tahir and Arndis to join them. They smoothed their clothing, smiled, and looked very happy.

Freyja went to the barn to get Lek and Red Eric (the other Eric on their ship was called Short Eric). Lek pulled on his blond beard and nodded to Eric as he walked past him. He walked ahead as if he could not wait to eat. Red Eric walked slowly and reached out to put his arm around Freyja's shoulders. She fit under his arm very naturally. She breathed deeply as if she could breathe him into her body.

They spoke quietly about the weather and the colors of the sky portending a good end to the harvest.

They gathered to sit at the table on benches to share stew, warm from the pot. Nora had made fresh flat bread and Tahir pulled out a wine skin for them to try the red liquid from the southern grapes. Nora and Brigit had had wine before and liked it. Arndis tried it, but poured half of her cup into Freyja's as she wanted no more. Freyja found that it made her thinking foggy, not unlike mead, and was enjoying it a little too much. Tahir and his men told stories of their adventures. It was hard to tell if they were true or exaggerations, but they were very entertaining. There was much laughing until Tahir found the wine skin empty.

"This is a sign that the gods want us to say good night. Thank you for the *nattmal*," said Tahir as he took Arndis by the hand, pulling her up off the bench toward him, a bit unsteadily. She adjusted his path to pull him to the room that was now Freyja's and hers. Arndis winked at her daughter with a smile. Freyja was happy for her mother, remembering the love the two had shared last spring.

Nora busied herself with picking things up and Brigit went to bed. Lek stood up, stretched, and made his excuses to go to the barn. Nora asked Freyja to bank the coals and she left to bed as well.

In the soft fire light, Freyja looked at Eric. His red hair and beard made his blue eyes shine like stars on a dark night. His strength was that of a well-toned warrior. Arms sculpted by rowing and wielding a sword. He stood tall and pulled Freyja to stand. She felt drawn to him and reached up a hand to cup his cheek.

Eric turned his face to kiss her hand. "You should not be held by these walls," he whispered. "I will take you where you are free under the open sky."

He put one arm around her waist and the other under her knees to lift her up and carry her down the stairs, outside. She did not resist, but clung hungrily to him. She could feel his heart beating with hers as their chests touched.

He carried her toward the meadow and sat on a large bolder. She felt warm on his lap and a freeing laugh escaped her. He laughed in answer and held her close. Of the same mind, she turned to face him and knelt on his lap. Hands moved together to untie the neck of her underdress and pull it down over her shoulders. He buried his face in her breasts. His tongue searched to taste her. She raised her chin to the sky and arched her back. His mouth felt gloriously soft and warm upon her breasts, his hands upon her thighs.

Freyja felt a fire light between them. It was not the quick hot fire she had had with Sven, like flint to kindling. It was that of a lightning strike on the forest floor. Slow burning in the loam, ready to burst into an intense raging inferno. They both felt it building within and between them and gasped at the same time.

Freyja reached down to pull at Eric's tunic as he reached to pull up her skirts. They felt their thighs touch and just as being warmed by a fire on a cold day, they both shivered.

They sank into each other quickly and moved as one. Breathing together they rocked and made a soft music of pleasure.

In moments, Eric rose and laid Freyja down upon the forest floor. They continued their love making until both sighed with joy. Freyja panted as she felt a full-body warm glow that she had never before experienced. Eric smiled to himself, well pleased that she was satisfied. He stood to retrieve his fur cloak left on the boulder, spread it out for them to rest upon, and gathered Freyja into his arms. Snuggled together they slept under the glittering silver stars.

They rested peacefully for hours until moonrise, when they both felt the pull of the tides and woke to start their love making anew. Freyja slid her hand down to search among their clothing. She found and encircled him with her eager hand. He quickly responded. Then she widened her own legs to slide her fingers between them. She moved her hand to ready herself and then rolled on top.

Straddled atop him, Freyja pleasured herself which then also pleasured him. They breathed rapidly and thrust together until they climbed their peaks of pleasure. Freyja rolled off Eric breathless and he pulled her close to kiss her deeply. They kissed and sighed contentedly. Eyes closed, they fell back asleep entwined blissfully around each other once again.

Chapter Twenty-Four

Freyja woke warm, encircled in Eric's arms. She looked up to see him watching her as she slept. She lowered her eyes a little embarrassed and he reached down to tip her chin up for a kiss. A long probing kiss. She smiled up at him then remembered that there were others on the farm. She gathered herself together and leaving him, crept into the house.

She went to Nora's bed and roused Brigit to hunt for eggs. "We have some men to feed," Freyja whispered.

Brigit mumbled, not enthusiastically, "All they do is eat."

Nora stretched and used her feet to push Brigit out of bed, while she giggled, "Oh they do so much more."

When Lek rose from the barn, the girls went in to milk the goats and cow then released them to the outside. Chores on the farm were always done before the morning meal as was tradition. They were thankful to share bread and butter and milk with left over stew from the night before, for their *dagmal*. Eric kept smiling at Freyja and she kept blushing. It was not wasted on Arndis who was suspecting something. "Now," said Tahir. "Show me what you know of fighting."

"Yes," said Arndis, "take your silly smiles elsewhere."

They all went to the flat ground by the forest edge where Tahir had come upon them yesterday. Tahir had the girls pair with his friends, Eric and Lek, and was pleasantly surprised. Their footwork was such that they were able to dodge the sword thrusts so Tahir thought the men were being too easy on them. "Fight now men!" he yelled. They doubled their efforts and the girls kept up. They practiced for quite a while and the girls ended up showing bruises on their hands and arms. When Tahir called, "Halt," he explained that with real swords those would be serious wounds or loss of limbs.

"I understand," said Freyja between gulps of air, "We are still learning."

"We will do more after a rest," Tahir said. But was instead he thought to use the spears.

He was eager to have them work with their spears and their targets. The men were able to show them some tricks to improve their accuracy.

Tahir then had them tear large pieces of bark from fallen trees to make into substitute shields. This was new to Freyja as she had not yet worked with a shield. She found it was a great advantage and took to it well. She loved being able to block a sword and then whirl about to smack her opponent from behind. She cheered loudly for herself. When Tahir called a stop to practice, Freyja was exuberant.

"You are right to be a shield-maiden, Freyja. You seem suited to it," Tahir said with pride.

"I hope to learn more and do well for my people," Freyja replied gasping to catch her breath.

"Now may we rest?" Lek asked Tahir. "I feel as if we have earned it."

Tahir laughed, "You have helped Freyja and Brigit learn and I thank you."

After a rest, Eric and Lek wanted to go to the village for the Mead House and maybe some trade. They gathered their things and began walking when Sven arrived on his horse. "I am to tell Arndis and Freyja that the Old One is coming," he yelled.

Arndis raced out of the house to ask, "She comes to cast the runes for Freyja?"

"Yes, she is coming now with many from the village."

Arndis ran inside, "Nora, make bread. Freyja check your snares. Brigit look for eggs and harvest vegetables. We need a feast." Tahir's friends turned around upon hearing there was to be a feast.

Tahir asked, "What is happening?" Arndis explained that the Old One was coming to cast the runes for Freyja to either bless or end her plan to become a shield-maiden.

"I will send to the ship for more dried fruit and wine. If they have an open bag of grain, I will buy it and they will bring that too. We will bless this endeavor with the gods' help." He sent the Lek and Eric to the ship and they retuned shortly with two more men in tow. In the meantime, the Old One arrived in a wagon with her family walking alongside. They brought dried meat and much mead. Freyja ran to help the seer out of the wagon and found more old friends inside. Hallr and Kofri smiled broadly as they climbed down.

"We bring your grandfather's weapons and if all goes well, they will be yours tonight," Hallr said with a wink.

Kofri looked around, "We hear there is wine here. Perhaps we can try it? Fereshte has called it potent." Freyja realized that the dark eyed woman had come with the Old One and the old brothers when she too emerged from the wagon.

Og and Helga came walking with several of Sven's friends. Helga looked around and sniffed with her nose in the air. "It seems a good farm even though it is of only a few women." She was surprised with the farm. She had been sure it would be poorer since Arndis had given up her profession. She would have to find something else to have against the woman who had once, long ago, been her childhood friend.

When Arndis asked for help to bring out the table and benches Karle uncharacteristically volunteered. Karle always enjoyed a party and this would be a feast as well. Besides, his entourage of young girls was watching. They batted their eyes at him and tittered as he showed off how helpful he could be. "Arndis, is there else that I can help you with?" When she turned her back to him to point at something the girls rushed to surround him and he waved his arms and led them off in the other direction. No doubt telling tall tales of his journey with Freyja to Rocky Peak to find items for the recent Harvest *blot* to the god *Freyr* and the goddess *Freyja*.

Karle had been a lifelong friend of Sven and was a grandnephew of the Old One. He often used these connections to his advantage when it suited him. He had proven himself not to be of much help when he accompanied Freyja on her journey to find gifts for the gods. At the time, most of the men were on a viking so her choice had been limited.

With the help of many hands, a fire was built outside and the cooking irons brought out. Stew was started and the mead began to be shared. The Old One and the old brothers were given seats of honor, even padded with furs. The seat of the Old One was made higher for her honored station as *volva*, or seer.

As the sky was turning amber with the promise of a setting sun, the people gathered around the Old One like moths to a just-lit flame. She had Freyja draw a circle in the dirt and surround it with bones. She asked Freyja to place something that was important to her in the center. Freyja knew immediately that it would be her coin necklace. She untied the leather thong from around her neck and started to place it in the circle. The Old One snatched it from her hand and put it in her mouth. She sucked on it for a moment then pulled it out to throw it into the circle herself. She began to sway as she slowly stood. She reached for her bag of runes. She whispered her incantations then closed her eyes, breathed into the bag, and dumped the runes out. Most landed within the circle.

The Old One opened her eyes and knelt slowly to touch and read the runes in her sing-song voice. "Weapons from the old days will take you into the future. Your father's daughter will be your teacher. Listen for your goddess, *Freyja*, not only in matters of love. Love will come and go until silver ransoms your heart. Listen to your grandmother when she whispers in your ear. Remember, 'When Freyja and Sven couple and children are born then we will trade with many and our village will prosper'" Freya's face showed confusion at this and she looked at Sven. He smiled nervously and looked away.

"Odin welcomes you as a shield-maiden," the old woman's voice rang out loudly as she raised her face to end her reading. The people cheered wildly upon hearing the ruling on Freyja's welcome as a shield-maiden.

The cheering was interrupted. "Do you know enough or will you have more?" the Old One shouted pointing a crooked finger at Freyja. The mood darkened and all looked to Freyja. She swallowed hard and knew that she must commit fully to her new journey.

"I will know," she lifted her chin and took a deep breath.

The Old One's hand went up and they quieted. "The outside of the circle is to be read. These pieces here say that the dark trader must go on the ransom trip." Everyone looked at Tahir. "He will serve as the right hand of Og,"

Tahir looked surprised then threw up his hands. "Who am I to challenge Odin." The Old One squinted her eyes and looked down her nose at him. "Or the Old One," added Tahir with a wink. His brown eyes twinkled and he flashed his brilliant Moorish smile at the Old One. She was completely disarmed as all women had been, in Freyja's experience.

"I will go and my share of new trade profits will stay with Arndis until my return." There were mumbles of approval. Everyone cheered even more when Tahir pulled out the wine skins. Then the feast began in earnest.

The old brothers brought out the weapons of Freyja's grandfather and showed all how they had sharpened and repaired them. Everyone admired them and the elders related stories of her grandfather to Freyja. The toasting and singing continued long into the night. The village folk were at their best. Feasting, laughter, and stories filled the hours. Friendly embraces came often and fighting was only for fun.

The Old One was given a warm bed and many couples found a place under the stars for their love making. Arndis took Tahir to her bed with the intensity of a good-bye now that she knew he would go along on the spring ransom voyage. She knew he had planned to be leaving to another village soon, but this change brought about the possibility of dangers for him. She intended to surround him sufficiently with her love and protection all winter so that he might carry it within his heart on the voyage.

Gunnar had come back from the village with the others and he and Nora had been inseparable the whole night. Freyja assumed they could be found in Nora's bed till sunrise. Lek and Fereshte spent much time together during the feast and perhaps later. Their light and dark hair made them a handsome couple. Freyja lost track of Brigit and though she worried because Sven was there also, her focus was on her own passions with Red Eric.

Freyja and Eric returned to the meadow, hand in hand, to rekindle the spark of the previous evening. On the ground they made a nest of the furs they carried. Free of their clothes they felt the pull of their hearts under the furs and pressed their bodies together to feel those hearts beat. Cool skin was quickly warmed as they clung together. Their chests heaved with the intake of cool air. Eric's breath warmed Freyja's neck as he began kissing his way to her mouth. Each mouth hungered for the other's and joined in passionate kissing.

Freyja energetically threw her leg over Eric's to gather him toward her. With the movement one of his hands quickly grasped her thigh. He reached between her legs with his other to massage her. She responded pushing into his hand. Her breath came quickly as she moved to climb on top of him. She captured his hips and surrounded his firm flesh with her own. The two moved in rhythmic passion, then flipped over for more. Freyja felt as if the furs must belong to her own body as her animal satisfaction peeked. For his part, Eric gave himself in movements that met hers so that they crumpled at the same time with sighs of surrender in the moonlight. Another wonderful night of love making was theirs.

Chapter Twenty-Five

The morning brought change with a light dusting of snow. Those who slept outside stood to shake snow from their furs and stomped their feet in the chill air. They clapped their hands together and hugged for not only gratitude of passion, but also for warmth.

The village folk packed up for home. The elders of the group were fed first and helped back into the wagon. Fereshte went with them after a smoldering look with mumbled goodbye to Lek. Og and Helga hobbled home, realizing that it had been long since they had slept on the ground, but happy for the celebration. Og had gotten much praise for his upcoming journey and Helga had gotten many offers of help while he was away.

Sven and his friends helped to clean up with Brigit, though of course Karle had managed to slip away. Arndis had to shoo the group away when she ran out of things for them to do. She knew if they stayed too long, they would need to be fed again. Sven especially seemed to want to linger, but Freyja added her disapproving look to Arndis' when he was asked to leave.

Tahir said that he, Lek, and Eric would go to the ship and get goods to trade in the village and Gunnar decided to go along. They would give all the crew some time in the village before they would take their ship home for the winter.

Red Eric was not sure he would see Freyja again, but he would keep her in his heart. "You are indeed like the goddess of love and passion. You have made me feel like a welcome warrior. May you bring much wealth to your people." Lek shared an approving look with Eric and nodded to Freyja.

"Perhaps we will meet again, Red Eric," Freyja said and held his hands, then let finger by finger slip away. It was not a sad goodbye. She now knew that she could love again. Her heart had not turned to stone with the loss of Sven's love. She smiled as the men left.

All was quiet and it felt strange, but they soon returned to a more normal routine. The women tended to the animals and decided on quiet time. Nora and Arndis both went to their beds. Freyja assumed they needed to catch up on their sleep. Brigit busied herself making butter and cheese, all the while humming and smiling wistfully. Freyja shook her head as she watched her. Feeling the need to get away, she took a walk.

She found herself in the meadow, walking to her altar. She brushed off dirt, leaves, and needles from the ledge and around her grey stone and the black stone of Brigit. Neither they nor the gods spoke to her. She turned to look at the forest and was drawn to a young cedar tree. She built a small fire in the clearing near it and once the flames were showing she added some dried cedar branches. Standing over the fragrant smoke, she pulled it toward her and bathed in it to purify herself.

"Sacred flame, cleanse me. Hail, *Blotgydja*. I ask for your protection and guidance on my journey as a shield-maiden. Teach me your *seidr* magic so that I may forever bring honor to your name, *Freyja*," she chanted. She sat on the forest floor, quietly watching the flame. She remembered what the Old One had said, "Listen for your goddess *Freyja*, not only in matters of love."

She had often sought the advice of the goddess when she was looking for the love of Sven. She had begged the goddess to fulfill the prophecy by mating with Sven. She had asked for much, but not offered in return. She had truly neglected her devotions since Sven had been removed from her future. She now felt guilty that she should have forgotten the goddess for whom she was named.

"But I have not forgotten you. I will never leave you," she heard the voice plainly.

"I have brought no offerings to give you. No gold, nor silver. Not even mead to share today," Freyja said sorrowfully. She frowned and shook her head slowly.

'You forget that you are my name-sake. You are my gift and as long as you honor yourself, you honor me for it is said 'a gift looks for a gift.' Freyja felt a warm wind engulf her, almost like a hug. She felt a surge of energy rush from her core out through the top of her head as her chin tilted upward. Her breath filled her with a tingle that made her silently giggle

and at the same time bring tears. Emotions filled her. Tears began to fall as she let go of all her disappointments.

She now felt free in many ways. She was no longer tied to Sven. She no longer had a standing in the community because of the prophecy. She no longer had a guaranteed marriage. Everyone knew that she and Sven had bedded before he left on the viking. Now she would have to make her own reputation.

More tears fell as she questioned her future. She was confused. Somehow, she was still expected to participate in the fulfilling of the prophecy, but she had now fully committed to protecting her people as a shield-maiden. People had accepted the change to the prophecy from the Old One. They had also accepted her new role as shield-maiden as read from the runes. But what was she to do? How would she make these things happen? She had no plan about her path or steps forward.

She closed her eyes and *Freyja* sent her a vision; she saw her feet on a straight path that seemed to have no end. A feeling of exhaustion filled her, weighing down her shoulders. Just as she felt she would sink to the ground and give up her journey, the path turned into a spiral. She stood up, eager to travel around each bend, filled with excitement for her future and joy for the evolution of her life. She could not see around the bends, did not know what her path would bring, but she felt happy to trust *Freyja*, her goddess to guide her.

Her vision ended and she experienced a warm feeling of ease and belonging. She sat peacefully for a long time, watching the flames, as the fire died down. Her tears had dried upon her face. *Freyja's tears*, her gift to and from the goddess. She smiled and stood with a sense of calm and new purpose. Her feet started toward the creek.

Chapter Twenty-Six

The earth crunched under her feet when she stepped in the shadows. The sun was melting ice and frost still left on the path. It was the mark of changing to winter. She pulled her fur cloak around her and shivered slightly. As she neared the creek bank, she spotted two river otters playing. They slid down the natural berms on the bank into the water. Twirling and diving, they raced each other. Streams of water ran off their fur and glistened in the sun. They ran up the bank to slide down again, wrestling and tumbling as they went. Their joy was obvious and even contagious. Their chatter loudly filled the air.

Freyja sat on a nearby rock and watched them. She felt they were a vision of *Hnoss* and *Semi*, the goddesses of sisterhood, and laughed aloud. They startled, chirped at her, and swam away. Of course, the goddess *Freyja* would remind her not to forget the bond with her half-sister. They still had training to complete, together, on her journey to becoming a shield-maiden. The Old One had said, 'Your father's daughter will be your teacher.' Perhaps the otters were also a reminder to find joy in their work as well. Their playfulness made her smile and inspired her.

Freyja stood and stretched with a smile. She closed her eyes and tilted her face toward the sun. The focused warmth filled her with new life and happiness. The walk back to the farm seemed short and she delighted in the crunching sounds under foot, dancing a rhythm with her steps. When she got to the house she rushed to her weapons.

They were still wrapped in the sheepskin as returned by the brothers. She carried the skin outside and laid it on a stump. Untying and opening the bundle sent shivers of anticipation running through her. Her hand hesitated.

She picked up the axe reverently and admired the new leather bindings and smooth wooden handle. The edge had been finely sharpened. It felt heavy in her hands and she knew she had much practice ahead of her, in order to wield it well. The sword also felt heavy compared to her wooden practice one. Again, her arms would need to be strengthened. She lifted the dagger and clasped it in her hand. It shone in the sunlight, the facets of its edges glittering as she turned it. A question came to her about the wearing of it. Should she now wear it at her waist and let go her woman's knife? She would need a belt to carry her sword, and sheaths for both dagger and sword, as well. She traced with her finger the hammered image of Freyja's cats on each of the weapons, and silently thanked her grandfather for his gifts. Using these gifts would honor her ancestors.

She wondered why the shield of her grandfather had not been returned, but she had not asked about it during the gathering. She was sure to find the old brothers at the Mead House and would reclaim it.

Brigit came down the steps to stand near her sister. She marveled at the weapons that now belonged to Freyja. "The old brothers did well. These are as new," she said, touching each reverently. "You must do your best to honor your grandfather and his gift."

"Yes," replied Freyja. "Let us go to the village tomorrow to see if we might find a sword for you too, so that we might spar together."

Brigit directed, "For now we will make stick men to fight." Freyja laughed with a snort. Brigit looked at her seriously, "We make men of sticks to practice on. We can see where on a body our blows will land." Freyja nodded and followed Brigit to the edge of the forest where they had set targets before. Brigit began to gather sticks and such long grasses and vines that she could find in the early winter. Freyja followed her lead and did the same until they had each a huge bundle.

"Now we shape them into men and we can stand them up." They both laughed at their stick men, but created workable statues. By sundown there were two men standing at the end of the clearing. They laughed and talked as they went to the well to wash up after their work.

Arndis yelled out the door to them, "Come inside and help with *nattmal*. We still have food from the feast." Both girls shook the water from their hands and went inside. Nora was looking gloomy as Gunnar had gone to the village, but started to chat with the others as they enjoyed a good meal. Arndis found that they still had wine, which made Nora perk up even more.

"We go tomorrow to the village to find a sword for Brigit's training. Do not drink all of the wine for it will be a good trade," said Freyja with a warning frown at Nora.

Nora's face lit up, "Gunnar and Tahir will be in the village, Arndis. Let us go with them," she broached hopefully.

"Yes, we may as well all go. Let us gather together all we have to trade for this sword and perhaps some food and mead for the night," Arndis smiled at Nora and patted her hand. Nora was used to the coming and going of love. She had found the comfort of Gunnar to be a welcome surprise in this strange land and she was not happy to lose it even for a night.

Freyja thought also that the ship that had brought Tahir might still be at their shore which would mean that Eric would be in the village. The traders' business was not something that could be planned. Goods may be wanted, but then again barters may not be negotiated successfully. She hoped all had gone well and smiled in anticipation.

The women gathered bundles in preparation for their journey to the village and planned to leave at first light. Freyja had taken the full wine skin and tucked it in her bundle early in the evening and had let Nora sip from the one that was almost empty. Nora had enjoyed it and the women had enjoyed Nora's good humor as she talked about seeing Gunnar. She spoke of his shoulders and strong arms and how he held her in the night. She got so carried away that she stopped, looked at the girls, and broke into giggles that she could not stop. Arndis left to her bed as did Brigit. Freyja sat with Nora, as she giggled, staring into the hearth fire. She wondered if she would ever love in such a way as to let herself be so silly.

Chapter Twenty-Seven

Freyja stretched and stirred as the first fingers of sunlight reached across the sky. She nudged her mother to wake and childishly hugged her as she used to. "I will care for the animals," she whispered to Arndis.

As the sun broke over the tree tops, Freyja milked the cow and goats. Freyja would offer fresh cow milk to the women, starting their day at the fire. The goat milk would be saved for cheese. Brigit came out to gather eggs. She put them in her bundle to take to the village as they always made for a good trade.

To answer her question of Eric's ship remaining, Freyja ran to the rocky prominence to look for the visiting ship. She could see men loading it and preparing it to leave. Some were untying ropes even before everything was loaded, as if they were in a hurry to cast off. It seemed that her goodbye to Eric yesterday was indeed that last time she would see him. The traders must have concluded their trading in only one day. She thanked the gods for the love making that they shared and silently wished Eric safe travels in the days ahead of him.

She clambered down from the prominence and met the women with their bundles in hand, ready to go to the village. "The ship of Eric readies to leave," Freyja offered with a bit of a frown.

"I thank them for bringing Tahir back to me," Arndis said. She pursed her lips and nodded her head.

"I thank them for bringing wine," said Nora with a smile. "And you, Freyja? Do you thank them for bringing a man to steal your heart?" Nora's eyes twinkled and she winked at Freyja. Freyja just smiled and helped Nora up on the horse. This was a message from her goddess to focus on her training to become a shield-maiden. She would take heed.

She made a list in her head as they walked to the Mead House to find the old brothers and retrieve the shield. She would then start with them, to ask about a sword for Brigit. They might even help her with training. It seemed she was most in need of the brothers.

When they arrived in the village, Og was outside yelling loudly about thieves. "Those friends of Tahir robbed me," Og glared at Tahir.

"I only just met them at Hedeby. They were newly friends and I cannot vouch for their honesty," said Tahir sadly shaking his head.

Freyja interrupted as she helped Nora down from the horse, "What happened?"

"The traders came from your farm yesterday morning, as did we all. They sent men to the ship to bring wine and other things they had to trade. They sold wine to Halig, the owner, then drank most of it in sampling," Og offered incredulously.

"That sounds like thirsty men, but may not have been intentional," Freyja hoped she was right.

"Then," Og went on, "They wanted to trade for Helga's amber necklace. It is her own Brísingamen and she did not want to part with it no matter how much they offered. We were kind to let Lek stay at our home last night and when we awoke the necklace was gone and so was Lek." Helga was sniffling.

"So, then one of them was a thief to be sure." Freyja was relieved it had not been Eric.

Halig came outside of the Mead House on hearing this, with his hands on his hips. "The small barrel of wine we had left is gone." Fereshte came out and whispered in his ear. "And so is the silk that Fereshte traded for. It was in the back next to the wine."

Og started yelling about going after them and fighting for what had been stolen. "We do not know where they have gone," Gunnar pointed out. "Do you know, Tahir?" Gunnar asked. Everyone looked at Tahir a little suspiciously.

"I swear by Odin, I know nothing of these men. I was only to come here with them and perhaps continue trading with them. You must believe me. My desire was only to be in your village," he looked at Arndis. Arndis came to his side.

"I believe you, Tahir," replied Og. "I have fought beside you and have known you to be forthright." Og put his arm around Tahir's shoulders. "When we cross paths with them again, we will make things straight, Helga. I promise," said

Og while taking Helga in his other arm. Og steered them inside the Mead House.

Inside, all gathered at tables and began to talk about their departure in spring to the Far Isle. Sven came inside at that time to tell them that he had been down at the shore. "The ship broke up the ice further on their leaving," Sven said. He sat in front of the fire and rubbed his cold hands together. "I could not see their sail."

"They were leaving at first light when I saw them from the signal fire on our farm," Freyja spoke up. "They looked as in a hurry to leave. Casting off lines while still loading." Sven acknowledged Freyja with a serious nod. "I would not believe that they would steal from us who would so freely give," she said softly.

Nora patted her hand, "And would you not?" She had a thoughtful look on her face as if she herself had learned the lesson of giving love without reciprocity before.

Karle's mother and father bustled in the door followed by their children. "Karle? Is Karle here? Has anyone seen my son?" his mother asked hysterically. She looked around wildly. "When we awoke Red Eric and Karle were both gone. Karle must have been forced to leave. His things are gone!"

Helga related the story of Lek and her loss. "Karle may have been taken, just as my necklace. Only the gods know if he will become a slave." Helga uttered these words softly, but with a dreadful tone so that Karle's mother had to hand her newborn to Helga and sit down unsteadily. Both women began to weep and console each other. Their husbands looked very uncomfortable with the attentions of the whole hall upon them.

Og steered Karle's father by the arm away from the blubbering women and toward the group of men organizing the outfitting of the ship. They were stopped in their tracks by the entrance of the Old One.

"Deceit and desecration!" she shouted. Her son and grandchildren surrounded her as they settled her to a bench. "The god post of *Freyja* has been destroyed and her *blot* treasures taken," she wailed.

Freyja ran to her to kneel at her feet. "What are you saying?"

"The god post was chopped down with an axe. Her necklace was taken and her *seax* dug up," the Old One panted. The necklace and *seax*, long knife, had been given to Freyja when she had encountered the spirit of a shield-maiden who had owned them. She had earned them in trade for putting the wight to rest and ensuring her passage to *Vallhalla*.

"But no one knew of these things. Isn't this so?" asked Freyja. She noticed that all had quieted to listen to her and the Old One.

The Old One looked around at the people gathered, but spoke to Freyja. "My family was asked to place the necklace and bury the *seax* at the god post." She looked down, ashamed. "My son had the help of Karle."

Karle's mother sucked in her breath sharply. "Karle would do no such thing. He must have been tortured to reveal these items to Eric. He is surely a captive as are these items, now in the hands of raiders." She sobbed uncontrollably.

Helga was crying over the loss of her necklace. Karle's mother was crying over his disappearance. The Old One was crying with shame over the desecration of *The Lady's* items of *blot*. Freyja ran to get them each a cup of mead and patted their shoulders as she gave them out.

The old brothers arrived in the middle of this mayhem and Freyja left the crying women to meet them at the back door. They had stopped to learn of the news from Halig.

They moved to sit at their usual table and Freyja followed. "I did not ask you of the shield of my grandfather yet," she said quietly.

"Ah, yes." Hallr said. "We repaired the metal boss, brace, and rim, but some of the wood and the leather strap needed to be replaced."

"Our friend is doing that now," added Kafri.

"We can bring it to you when it is finished. We like your mother's cheese," Hallr smiled with many missing teeth. "We can help with your training, as well."

"I would welcome your advice," Freyja smiled at them. "My sword and axe are new to me and seem heavy."

"It is well. They will make you stronger," chuckled Hallr as he squeezed her forearm. His eyes twinkled between his white eyebrows and beard.

"Brigit is working with me, but against the weapons of my grandfather her wooden sword will no longer stand. Are you able to find some weapons for her to use or train with?"

Freyja looked at the brothers expectantly. The brothers looked at each other and nodded together.

"We have such things at our forge. You will come with us and look," said Hallr.

They stood and Freyja went over to pry Brigit away from the table which now held Sven as well. She grabbed Brigit's arm. "We will go now to look at weapons for you."

Brigit glowered at her until the words made sense to her. "Oh, yes. I will go with you." She stood from the table and followed Freyja and the brothers.

It was the first time since Freyja was a child that she had been to the forge. She remembered only that there had been many tools about and that it had been hot. Now she saw evidence of the beauty of the art. Pieces of metal were in various stages of becoming tools or weapons. In one corner she noticed an altar with a god post. She knew right away that it must be the god *Wayland* as he is the god of metalworking. There was evidence of offerings and she believed that the brothers made their *blots* often.

Hallr reached under a table and brought out an axe. It was obviously older, but kept in good repair. "Will this do?" he asked Freyja.

She held it up to get a better look at it. A great smile crossed her face. "Yes, this is wonderful. Brigit, hold it and see. We will use it well and return it."

"No need," replied Hallr. "Kofri and I are past days of fighting and besides we have others for protection."

Kofri pulled a sword from a corner and handed it to Brigit. "Same with this one. It served me well, but I have others,"

Kofri smiled. "We feel fortunate for our weapons that they will enjoy more use and perhaps even battle."

"Thank you. We sisters will honor them and you brothers as well. When you come to the farm, we will feed you well and you may guide us further in our training. Thank you," Freyja said with much sincerity.

"And now, to go back to the Mead House," Hallr gestured for all to leave and Kofri was first out with a happy step.

Brigit and Freyja each carried a weapon back to the table and laid them down. Fereshte saw them enter and filled a cup for each of the brothers, bringing them right away. Her eyes fixed on the weapons and she drew in her breath. Kofri took the cups and nodded at Freyja and Brigit and said a few words. Fereshte nodded but still looked at the table. Her eyes glistened and she reached out with her left hand to caress the handle of the axe. She reached for the sword with her right hand and her fingers began to close around the hilt. Kofri made a noise in his throat, looked at the woman, and shook his head fiercely. He did not want anyone to get the wrong idea. If a slave had a weapon in their hand, much less could wield it as Fereshte could, it might very well mean death. Kofri gestured with his chin toward the jars and barrels, "Mead for Freyja and Brigit," he said softly. Fereshte stood, as if in a dream, and made her way to the back to fill the cups.

When the woman came back, she sat down next to Freyja and asked questions with her eyes. "The brothers," Freyja gestured toward Hallr and Kofri, "have given Brigit these to use for fighting." Freyja pointed at Brigit and then at the weapons and pantomimed their use. Fereshte giggled at Freyja's movements, but nodded in understanding.

"Yes," said Fereshte. "You?" and she pantomimed the use of the axe and sword.

"Yes," said Freyja. "I train with weapons also, but have those of my grandfather." Fereshte nodded, but Freyja was not sure she had understood. Kofri interjected some words and Fereshte nodded.

Fereshte sat with them, listening and looking longingly at the weapons, until Halig saw her and scolded her. "Find some useful work to do," he growled, but he did it with a smile.

"Those two have a strange bond," began Kofri. "When he defeated her in battle, she was a warrior. If she had been a man, he would have killed her. As you know, because of his respect for her, he has promised that at the end of eight years or his death, she shall have her freedom."

"And her weapon," Hallr pointed to the wall near the ladder to the loft. Way up high hung a scimitar next to its sheath. The hilt of the sword was wrapped in a soft green fabric that blew with the breeze.

Brigit and Freyja admired the gifts of the brothers and thanked them again and again, vowing to make them proud. Arndis came to the table with Tahir's hand in hers and a great smile upon her face, "We are to the farm," said Arndis. Freyja smiled, glad that her mother was happy.

"Good night, Freyja," said Tahir. They headed toward the door and Freyja could see that the sun was just beginning to set. She found Nora to tell her that she and Brigit were going back to the farm, but Nora wanted to stay with Gunnar, and Freyja could see no harm in it. At this point Nora and Brigit had ceased being captives and had become part of the family, truly.

Brigit packed her weapons on the horse and she and Freyja walked slowly toward the farm. When Freyja looked back, she saw Sven looking forlorn as he watched them leave. If only he had ever looked at her in such a way she thought and the corners of her mouth twisted wryly. She sighed at this musing, then threw off the thought. He had never felt as she. She understood this now and wondered if the prophecy would have ever unfolded as she had hoped. Now she and Sven had independent missions in order to fulfill the prophecy. Still, she wondered about the ways and means to make this possible.

Brigit was looking forward and did not see Sven nor notice Freyja looking back. She was chatting about the new weapons she would train with and how they should create some protective clothing in case they were not always accurate or in control. "My wrists have bruises from the wooden swords, we must be very careful with the use of these weapons as we train. We should work first with our stick men and when we get better against each other. Oh, Tahir is at the farm for the winter. We will ask his help. Yes?" she looked to Freyja for some input. "Yes? Are these good thoughts?" Brigit asked.

"Oh, yes," replied Freyja. "Very good thoughts." They walked the rest of the way in quiet.

Freyja took care of the horse when they got to the farm and Brigit looked at her weapons again. "Freyja, bring your weapons out so we may look on them together."

"They have not changed Brigit. They look the same as they did yesterday," Freyja snapped. Seeing Sven looking at Brigit had set her teeth on edge and her voice sounded so. Freyja looked at her sister to see a look of great pain on her face. "Oh Brigit, I am tired. I will do this in the morning, but now I feel the need of my altar." Freyja walked toward the meadow leaving Brigit looking after with questions on her face.

Freyja sought the comfort of her goddess, *The Lady*, for whom she was named. She longed for the feeling of acceptance and love that she knew was offered when she only asked. So, she did. "Hail to *Freyja*, goddess of cat-chariot and falcon wing cape. Hail to *Mardoll* of the blue ocean depths. Hail to *Blotgydja* of sacrifice duty. Hail to *Vanaheim's flower*, Hail V*anadis!*" Freyja reached for her carved stone as she spoke the many names of her goddess. "I bring my own *blot* to you today as I pledge myself to you." She took her knife from its sheath and cut her finger to bring the blood. She decorated her stone with her blood. "May this *blot* please you." She then placed her stone on the center of the altar and stood with open arms. "I come to you once again, F*reyja*, to ask for your guidance in my life. Be welcome in my life, my home, and my altar which now belong to you. I ask for your continued guidance on my journey as a shield-maiden." Freyja sat on the earth and did not have to wait long.

"You must be quiet to hear guidance. The All-Father and we watch you with joy. I will be near when you need me. Not only in matters of love, but in life. Now rest in seidr."

Freyja felt a great heaviness in her eyes and closed them to fall into a trance. Again, she saw the hall *Sessrumnir* and she was the goddess. She was at the door to greet the fallen warriors she had chosen. Many looked familiar and were led by Eric. He approached her with one arm open and a look of love. As he drew near and she reached for him, he pulled a sword from behind his back to attack. She was quick to respond and swept his legs from under him as she ducked and rolled beneath his blade. From behind him she quickly pulled her dagger across his neck and pulled his sword from his hand. The others watched in horror as she would not return his blade to his hand, but let him die without his weapon in his grasp. Freyja whistled and the black hound, *Garm,* appeared followed by his mistress *Hel* to escort Eric to *Niflheim.*

Freyja felt her body shiver as she became aware of it again. Her legs had stiffened and the sky had darkened. She rose slowly and shook off the dark vision she had had. She could smell something cooking and see lights of the farm, so she slowly made her way there. She hoped she would feel something of herself once home and fed.

Arndis, Tahir, and Brigit were eating bread, rabbit, and herbs for their *nattmal* and chatting pleasantly. Freyja was welcomed and handed a bowl. They acted as if nothing was out of the ordinary. She ate quietly and nodded along with some of the chatter. Soon Arndis and Tahir disappeared hand in hand and Brigit went to her bed. Freyja sat next to the fire and watched it as it died. She felt a strange mixture of foreboding and strength. She knew the goddess would not show her things without showing her the way to succeed as well, and she was at peace.

Chapter Twenty-Eight

The first thing in the morning Freyja took out her weapons and laid them on the stump before going to milk the cow. Brigit soon joined her to hunt for eggs.

"I will bring my weapons out too after we eat *dagmal* and we can start our training," Brigit called gaily. She was searching under the chickens in the corners of the barn. "Now we have each a sword and axe. I am happy that we made our stick men already."

With all the milking done and eggs gathered the girls entered the house to find Arndis and Tahir sitting together eating bread and butter. "Here is milk also," said Freyja generously.

"This is good," said Tahir. "For we have an appetite." Arndis rolled her eyes, but smiled at him while he winked at her.

"Eat well. We have need of you to help us with our swords," said Brigit.

"We?" asked Tahir.

Brigit gushed, "Yes. The brothers have given me sword and axe. We have made stick men and are ready to fight."

"Let us hope that your stick men are not too fierce," laughed Tahir after he had downed a cup of milk. He wiped his mouth on his sleeve and kissed Arndis. "I will see this for myself."

Tahir followed Freyja and Brigit to the edge of the forest to find their stick men tied to small trees. "This is well. Now to see you use your swords." He had both sisters handle their swords and attack their respective stick man. They were clumsy in their attempts and he asked them to think about when they might be doing this.

"I will use my sword to protect as I have sworn," answered Freyja.

"So, let us do what we might to stop an attacker." Tahir pointed out vulnerable body parts on the stick men and worked on how they would proceed. "Grasp your wrist with your other hand and attack with the front edge of the sword." They practiced several hours.

"My wrist is hurting," Brigit said as she leaned on her sword. She shook her arm and winced.

Freyja panted, "We could stop?" She looked at Tahir hopefully.

"Alright," he said. "It is the first day, but later we will work with the axe." He nodded 'yes' and raised his eyebrows. Freyja got the distinct impression that he was not pleased with their skills. She bit her lip and looked at the ground. She dropped her sword and Tahir snatched it up quickly.

"This is not how to care for your sword. You should take them now to clean and sharpen." He marched the girls to the well where they took long drinks of the cool water and sat down to rest. "Now you will care for your swords as they are your children. Most have names and if they have belonged to others, they have history. You must care for them and they will care for you." Tahir showed them how to care for their swords and left them to go inside after getting his own drink of water. He was grumbling under his breath as he entered the house.

After a time, Tahir came outside. "Now for the axe." The girls brought them to their training place and Tahir showed them how to grip them.

"It seems that these axes are short," Freyja said with a question in her voice.

"Better for hiding," said Tahir. "These can be held behind a shield or hidden beneath a cape. These will do well for you." He had them try different approaches on their stick men and again they trained for several hours.

When they approached the house, Arndis came out on the step to tell them to care for the animals. Tahir interrupted, "They must care for their weapons first then they may." Arndis' hands went to her hips and she breathed up tall, but held her tongue. The girls both looked at her for approval and she nodded. Tahir walked up the steps to put his arms around her waist and she laughed like a girl then pulled him inside.

This first day set their routine. Up with the frost to care for animals and *dagmal* near the warm fire. Then to train with swords and care for them. After a break they went back to training with their axes. When they were finished, they cared for their axes and the animals once again. With sunset coming earlier, they came inside for *nattmal* where they talked and listened to Tahir's tales of traveling.

Many days followed this routine and the girls were getting stronger and more skilled with both weapons. Tahir showed them how they could spar with the swords for practice without hurting each other. He would test them often and they would get a slap with the flat of his sword. No blood was drawn, but there were welts to be sure. "You might make protection of bear or wolf skins, like *Odin's berserkers*, so the sword won't bite," Tahir joked with them

Freyja knitted her eyebrows and looked like she was thinking deeply about this, then replied, "Ah, but we are clever and want *Freyja* to choose us for her hall, *Sessrumnir*, in *Folkvangr* rather than *Vallhalla*. We will learn clever ways of protection." As the days got colder, they put on more clothes and the welts were fewer, but they were also less swift and adept with their movements. They needed to work much harder and receive more and greater trainings in order to become worthy of a place in *Sessrumnir*.

This was now a new goal for both sisters, but other thoughts tugged on Freyja's heart. How would she fulfill her part of the prophecy?

Chapter Twenty-Nine

Each morning there was a growing layer of ice to break up on the water's surface at the well. They were glad they had stored up much firewood. Tahir had the sisters chop even more using the farm axes to work on their war techniques and though they worked up a sweat, their wrists no longer ached.

Tahir made a rough sledge and they used the horse to pull it to the neighboring farm. The twin girls' father was looking to trade his abundant hay. The hay would help Arndis' farm overwinter the cows and goats successfully. They brought cheese and fermented roots with them, as well as squirrel and rabbit pelts. Tahir also insisted in bringing the last of his dried fruits. It turned out well as the father was happy to add some mead to the trade because of the "exotic" fruits.

"Freyja," said the neighbor mother as she pressed a bag into her hand. "Your mother has told me that your shawl is in need of repair. Here is the same spun wool and a needle for *nalbinding*. I can teach you." She smiled warmly.

The neighbors were all in good spirits. They were starting their preparations for *Winter Nights* which marked the end of summer and the start of winter. As always, there would be three days of celebration and the *Vetrnaetr Blot* sacrifice. They had heard that Og would sacrifice a horse in thanks for the good harvest and to ensure an abundant one next year. They had even made a special ale for the *Sumbel,* the ceremonial drinking to the gods and elves. They were planning to go to the village on the next full moon. "We hope to see you all there. We will share a drinking horn with you to ensure a good season," the mother said as she hugged Arndis good-bye.

"We will be there. Tahir is getting too used to our feasts and I hope to surprise him," laughed Arndis. "Hail the gods! We are indeed looking forward to even more prosperity." She looked at Freyja with a proud smile and then quickly at Brigit with a melancholy smile.

Freyja noted the looks Arndis gave each girl and thought about the coming darkness and cold. They would train in the rough weather to fill the time while waiting for spring. Training would take Brigit's mind off of her return to the Far Isle and prepare Freyja to become a shield-maiden.

She walked with one hand holding the hay steady as it rocked on the sledge, bumping through bits of white ice clinging to the dark mud. Her thoughts went back to the only shield-maiden she had met.

The shield-maiden had been a skeleton warrior wrapped in a tattered disintegrating cloak that Freyja had discovered on Rocky Peak. When Freyja reached her hand to lift a glittering gold and amber necklace from the skeleton's neck, ice blue eyes materialized. The skull transformed with a covering of pale translucent skin and a woman's face appeared, eyes narrowed.

Freyja had made a bargain with the wight to keep the necklace of gold and amber as a gift for a *blot* to the goddess, *Freyja*. She was tasked to kill and bury the ghost's skeleton to ensure the spirit's journey to *Valhalla*. She was also sworn to secrecy about the fate of the warrior woman and for that the shield-maiden had given her a *seax*. Under a dark night sky, Freyja had dealt a death blow to the possessed skeleton and laid her back to die once more, upon the cold ground. At once the Northern Lights appeared and she witnessed the spirit rise to join the *Valkyries* riding across the heavens.

That necklace and the *seax* she had been given in trust had now been stolen by Red Eric's men. She battled with feelings of responsibility to the shield-maiden and to the goddess for the loss of these gifts. She felt a bitterness rise in her throat and knew that she must right this wrong.

Then she thought of Fereshte. The old brothers said that the beautiful Persian woman had been a shield-maiden in her culture. Perhaps she could learn more about such women.

Finally, she remembered her promise to use her grandfather's weapons to protect her people. She had made a pledge to many to become a shield-maiden. Her people were now invested in her through the vision of the Old One.

Once at the barn, they began to unload the hay. Over the next few days, they would return for even more, enough to fill the loft. It was dry work even though the ground around them was wet. Dust filled their nostrils and the air filled with golden sprites. It seemed that little spirits danced around them all until they had finished with today's load and the dust settled to the ground. The puddles now shone with a golden sheen.

Freyja ran out of the barn just as they finished, to take in huge gulps of fresh air. "By the gods, I am happy to breathe again," she gasped.

Brigit and Nora clapped each other on the back as they coughed to clear their lungs.

"Come to the well and wash," Arndis advised. They all straggled toward the promise of clean faces. Many hands reached into the bucket at once. The little bits of water they came out with went right to dusty eyes and mouths. "Now, now," said Arndis. "We will take our turns."

Hands and faces were relieved of the golden dust and mouths rinsed so that they could talk. As they passed around the bucket the coughing lessened.

Freyja looked down at one arm still covered in dust. "This golden color has me thinking of the necklace taken from the post of the goddess, *Freyja*, at the Old One's farm," she said with a worried frown. "I feel that the goddess may be angry with me." All of them shook their heads no.

"You could not know it would be stolen," said Arndis with a soothing voice.

"You had nothing to do with it," Brigit said while patting Freyja's hand.

"I also feel that the spirit of the shield-maiden may not be at rest because of the necklace, and the *seax*, as well..." Frejya's thoughts stopped.

Arndis furrowed her brows. "I heard the Old One whispering something of this with you. She was talking about Karle knowing of the gifts to the goddess. I, myself, do not know any more."

Freyja realized that she had said more than necessary. She was bound to keep the secret of the shield-maiden to protect her honor. "I have said too much," she said. "I am glad the neighbors prepare for *Winter Nights*. We are sure to have a good feast and you will all enjoy it." Freyja felt good about changing the subject and Arndis began to tell the others about their traditions.

They all shook out their clothes to enter the house. "I will check the snares," Freyja volunteered after they were all inside so that none would follow. A walk through the fresh forest air was just what she needed.

Her thoughts went to the days ahead, after the *Winter Nights* festivities. It was always fun, but then what? Freyja had experienced much in her young life, but still felt ill-equipped to meet what lay before her. She could not envision her future beyond a feeling of emptiness. She calmed her fears with the knowledge of life's cycles and that after the darkness light would return.

Freyja found two rabbits in her snares. When she got to the last one it also held a rabbit. She felt eyes watching her and looked through the branches as she knelt to kill the quarry. There was the she wolf with two pups. Their dark fur made her think of *Odin's* wolves, *Geri* and *Freki* as spoken of in the stories. She met the mother's eyes and threw the rabbit to her. "I gift you this rabbit, mother of pups, in *Odin's* name. Be well," Freyja called to her. The wolf picked up the rabbit in her mouth and bowed her head to Freyja as she slunk back into the dark green forest.

Freyja took the two rabbits to her meadow and bled them onto her altar as a *blot* to the gods. She stood in silence breathing deeply and gratefully. then closed her eyes, and deep within felt a tiny spark beginning to glow. It slowly warmed her from the inside, filling her up where she had felt empty. She lifted her face, eyes opened and shining with inner light. She would grow, like this spark, in power and force. There was more for her to do. She would fulfill the prophecy and her promises to her grandfather, her people, and the gods.

My Norse Prophecy fictional stories are inspired by Norse Pagan Gods/Goddesses and the traditions shared are those of the Viking Age. I have taken some license with variations of Germanic, Scandinavian, and Icelandic Pagan/Heathenism. My hope is that you will be encouraged to learn more for yourself through reading and research. My caution is that you be aware of groups and sources that may promote hate.

These stories are not intended to endorse White Supremacy, Supremacist or Nazi beliefs or practices. The travels of Viking Age Norse peoples took them around the world. They learned and borrowed from diverse cultures, especially through trade and intermarriage, thereby enriching their own culture. They sometimes settled in other parts of the world and brought their beliefs and culture to their adopted lands, as in the case of the Rus. Cultural diffusion was alive and well in those early times.

> "Odin is the All-Father,
> not the Some Father!"

Thanks to the historians and archeologists who work to improve our knowledge of the archeologic record of the Viking Age. Many thanks to Dr. Jackson Crawford and The Viking Answer Lady for cultural information of the Norse peoples. Tremendous thanks to my Beta Readers for their sharp eyes and even sharper tongues!

www.ingramcontent.com/pod-product-compliance
Lightning Source LLC
LaVergne TN
LVHW041710070526
838199LV00045B/1284